I0742652

IF WATER WERE

FIRE

ALSO BY SARA SALAM

My Truth Journal

Love Isn't Linear: A Collection of Poems About Modern Love

My Newport: A Collection of Poems About Newport Beach, CA

If Water Were Fire

Sara Salam

The Peacock Pen Press

2020

Copyright © 2020 Sara Salam

All rights reserved. No part of this book may be used or reproduced in any manner whatsoever without written permission, except in the case of brief quotations embodied in critical articles and reviews.

ISBN: 978-1-7337263-5-1 (Paperback)
ISBN: 978-1-7337263-6-8 (Hardcover)
ISBN: 978-1-7337263-7-5 (eBook)

Library of Congress Control Number: 2020906537

1. Coming of Age. 2. Friendship. 3. Family Dynamics.
4. Multiculturalism. 5. #Ownvoices. 6. Diversity. 7. Bullying.
8. Teen—Young Adult. 9. Wellness. 10. Mental Health.

This is a work of fiction. Names, characters, places, and incidents either are the product of the author's imagination or are used fictitiously, and any resemblance to actual persons, living or dead, businesses, companies, events, or locales is entirely coincidental.

Book cover design by Aspen Denita.
Front cover photography by Matt Hanlon.
Illustrations by Sara Salam.
Author portrait by Christina Wehbe.
Edited by Anna Alger.

Icons from the Noun Project:
Sailboat and Anchor by Mungang Kim.
Ocean by Olena Panasovska.

Printed by The Peacock Pen Press in the United States of America.

First Printing Edition 2020.

© 2020 Sara Salam
🌐 www.bysarasalam.com
📷 @bysarasalam
▶ Sara Salam

For my parents, Abdul and Janelle, who have shown me that love comes in all shapes, sizes, and colors, who have always done their best to help me feel safe and empowered, even in times when it doesn't seem possible.

CONTENTS

If Water Were Fire

Clouds clutter coastlines
turning blue star fields into painted skies.
A sun eases down, toward our simple, sweet
   town,
and disappears as its audience scatters away,
   gone.

A sultry glow lingers, at the tip of my fingers,
a veritable vixen of light hangs on to the
   cloud's wings.
If water were fire, flames would idle in ire—
the day is gone, and the night is on fire.

CHAPTER ONE
ACHAA

Labor Day dawns. It'll be a few hours before the lifeguard arrives at Tower 11 for his shift. For now, the waves crash unchaperoned.

This beachy locale is a haven for surfers. The south-facing shoreline makes an ideal wave for riding, Mother Nature permitting. Dry temperatures in the low eighties offer desirable beach weather for sunbathers, as well as the little ones sculpting sandcastles and digging for sand crabs.

I grew up here. This is my home.

While I am every bit the typical teenager entering her high school years, I'm also ... not. Unlike most of my peers, I've grown up in a multicultural family. Though I've been somewhat shielded from the outside world (i.e. the world beyond Newport Beach, California) and its (still) divided position on multiracial households, I write my own story, my own truth, amidst the highs and lows, the peaks and valleys of my reality.

My gal pals Charlie and Alex, my friends since sixth grade,

make their way down to the peninsula for one last hurrah before school starts.

Approximately 150 yards away, Papa Selim nests on our front patio, perched on his white lounge chair, afternoon tea in hand. His home of twenty years, he never passes up the chance to enjoy the ocean breeze.

My dad, Ashar, has led a legendary life. He was born in India, the exact date unknown due to the limited record-keeping methods of the time. He grew up alongside many brothers and sisters, most of whom passed early in life due to health complications. Access to healthcare was not readily available in their community at the time. After all, India, though industrial in many ways, identifies as a third world or developing nation.

His longest surviving brother, Akram, still lives at their family home with his wife, Shameem. Daddy and Akram talk on the phone all the time, truly a modern-day miracle.

Daddy's first language is Urdu, similar to Hindi in many ways. Both languages have the same origins, with similar grammar and phonology and many common words and foreign influences, including Arabic, Persian, and Turkic. Urdu is the national language of Pakistan while Hindi is the most commonly spoken language in India, though Urdu is also an official language of India. My dad's family migrated from India to Pakistan following India's split in 1947, for purposes of religious alignment.

I always thought the writing was so beautiful. While both languages are derived from Sanskrit, the Urdu writing system is called Nastaliq, which looks more like Persian and Arabic script and is therefore written from right to left. Hindi, on the other hand, uses the Devanagari script, which like English is written from left to right.

Before email, Daddy would write letters to Akram and Shameem in Urdu. It's like watching a calligrapher pen a wedding invitation, attuned to the detail and essence of the literal written word.

The first Urdu word I ever learned was *"achha,"* literally meaning "nice," but honestly in context it sounds like more of a filler word or acknowledgement, like English speakers might use *cool*, or *I see*, or *I understand*.

Sometimes I float around the house chanting *"achha"* because it sounds so melodic and is just fun to say, so distinctly a departure from how I speak outside my household.

Mama says Akram would call her *bhaabhii*, (pronounced like the name *Bobby*) which means "elder brother's wife." There's a word for essentially every family relation you can think of, unlike in English. For example, my mom's brother's son and mom's sister's son (if my mom had a sister) would both be considered my cousins, in English. In Urdu, however, the former would be my *mameraa bhaaii* and the latter would be my *mauseraa bhaii*. A subtle difference, yet a difference all the same, resulting in another term to commit to memory. I personally have *not* memorized each relation on my family tree and their corresponding epithet, though I do appreciate the personalization of the language. It's the earliest form of customization, this application of language. Today it seems like our focus is on customizing our homepages and social media accounts.

(On a somewhat related note, did you know that there are 125 MILLION people that speak English in India? That number is expected to quadruple in the next decade, and it will give India the largest number of English speakers of any country in the world. Crazy! The fluidity of language is fascinating.)

This aspect of my identity seems so far away from my immediate reality. While elusive in many ways, both tangibly and intangibly, it is so consciously present in the fabric of my life. As I readjust my Kashmari shawl on the sand, using it like a beach towel, I return my attention to said immediate reality.

"At least it's a nice day," Alex observes.

Truthfully, *nice* is relative. It's always *nice* in Newport.

"Are you ready for school to start?"

"Blah, ew, school. I'd prefer to take a class in tanning or picking up lifeguards. I would excel in those topics," shares Charlie, who is the least scholarly of the three of us. She might not be a virgin. I haven't asked her. And personally, I don't want to know.

"I'm curious about the new people," Alex responds. "I heard there's some transfers from the Catholic schools. They could be cute."

"Sure. And holy," I chide.

Sometimes I can be a smart ass. It's part of my charm.

The beach has only a few people this time of day. Eleventh street doesn't get a whole lot of riffraff, mostly because it's kind of far from any public restrooms or places to eat. Advantage, local people.

The unit, or the lifeguard patrol in the red pick-up truck, pulls up to the tower. Out jumps a scrawny dude, supposedly the relief guard i.e. the guy that gives breaks to the tower guards. He could be a rookie, it's hard to tell. He has a kind face, angelic and absent of fear.

The tower guard greets his relief and the unit operator before taking off into the water for a short swim. He'll resume his duties, a.k.a. babe-scoping, fifteen minutes later. But who's counting?

As the tower guard climbs back up into his lookout post, he pauses a moment, looking in our direction. At three half-naked girls sprawled out on beach blankets. Called that.

He's kinda cute. Short, bleach-blond hair, spiked back with seawater framing his sun-kissed face. His red trunks hang around the narrowest part of his body, exposing his butt dimples and leaving the rest to the imagination. He's not very tall, 5'10" is being generous, but you can tell he spends a lot of time at the gym. He has a nice back. I have a weakness for a well-defined back.

We overhear him chatting with his buddies.

"Dude, the swell is gnarly, brah," or something to that effect.

I wish I could say I was surprised by his word choice.

"Guys, I'm getting hungry. Want to go grab something from my house?" I'm starting to fade with the hazy sun. It's nearly 3 p.m.

"Nah, I think we'll just head home," Alex says. "School tomorrow. Oh joy."

"What are you wearing?" Charlie asks.

"Something cute," I reply.

"Well, duh, I figured. What kind of cute?"

"I was thinking *smart sexy chic*," I say, referring to my personal style.

"So, like, your Paige jeans and that off-the-shoulder top from Anthropologie?"

"You know me so well."

We wrap our towels around our hips—or in my case, my Kashmari shawl—and shake out our salty beach hair. I've never been an open water swimmer by any means, but there's nothing like a dip in a gentle ocean break.

We head towards the sidewalk that extends out from the street and make our way towards my house. Before I turn around, I catch a glimpse of the blonde lifeguard glancing in my direction. He's wearing sunglasses, so I can't see his eyes, but I'm confident he was looking at me. I think.

I quickly snap my head around and rush over to Alex and Charlie, who are already ten steps ahead of me.

"What's the matter?" asks Alex.

"Thinking about school just gave me a headache," I lie. I hate being called out for checking out boys. It makes me uncomfortable. And super awkward.

"I think she has a crush on Blondie over there," Charlie points out, referring to the tower guard.

"That must be it. Those red trunks really do it for me."

"Knowing you, I'd say it's his extensive vocabulary."

It's true. I'm a sucker for big words.

"The most complex word he said was 'gnarly,'" I defend. "Sounds promising."

"You never know."

CHAPTER TWO

PERSONAL PSYCHOLOGY

Here we are. Tuesday morning, the first day of high school. I can feel my stomach quease into knots, announcing the arrival of nerves and anxiety. I'm a pretty together person, but new social situations stress me out.

Not that today is an entirely new experience. I mean, I've been on this campus for the past two years and so at least I have that going for me. Truthfully, I'm more apprehensive about what I don't know. The *you don't know what you don't know* vibe. That business is hard to plan for. And I'm a planner.

Developing awareness around what you don't know is tricky, especially as a kid who literally doesn't know any better or have the benefit of anchored experience. Like, say, an adult.

Even adults have their moments.

I learned this abruptly when I was taking one of those standardized tests in fifth grade, the ones that the state uses to benchmark students' performance and subsequently rank each school. The scantron that collects personal information had an

EEOC (I didn't know what this was at the time: it stands for *Equal Employment Opportunity Commission*) question about race, or ethnic background. It's basically another dimension of statistics the government collects and uses to identify civic trends and generate reports.

There were six choices: White; Black or African American; Hispanic or Latino; American Indian or Alaska Native; Asian; and Native Hawaiian or Other Pacific Islander.

At the time, the choices didn't include *Two or More Races*—which, in hindsight, seems kind of silly. I have a handful of friends who experienced this dilemma, too. One friend's mom is Dutch, from Holland, and her dad is Mexican. A pair of my classmates, twins, are half Chinese and half German. I wonder what they put? It's an interesting social commentary on how the government views race overall.

I digress.

So, unsure of how to proceed, I asked the teacher what box I should fill in. I hardly ever ask teachers anything, yet for some reason the confusingness of this question compelled me to speak up. She looked really confused herself, and clearly didn't know how to answer the question, I presume for fear of being accused of offering her own social commentary on my ethnic heritage. I don't blame her; it's a charged and tricky post-9/11 time. But I was ten, the risk was pretty low.

She said, "Pick the one you most identify with."

That's a loaded question, one I'm still exploring five years later. How can you ask a ten-year-old that? How can you ask *anyone* that?

Perhaps as a reflection of my environment in this particular moment (my classmates are in fact 90% white) I select *White*. The next time we have a standardized government-issued test, though, I choose *Asian*. In my ten-year-old mind, it seems like the right thing to do, to select each answer half of the time. After all, I *am* half "White" and half "Asian" by the government's definition. (I am also technically 1/64, or 1.5% Sioux, the other kind of *Indian*, to add another twist to my dilemma.) Going forward when posed with this question, I alternate selections until *Two or More Races* becomes an option.

Despite these questions that (most of) my classmates would never encounter, I remind myself that I'm fortunate I'm not separated by land and sea from opportunities, educational and otherwise, like my dad was. And unlike my dad, my education is not financed by the sale of family property so that I can pursue the American Dream. His was, and he did. And here I am, encountering a uniquely different yet parallel set of challenges. At the ripe age of adolescence, I (hopefully) have a long way to go.

I wouldn't describe myself as shy, though some people might. I have an internal need to chat and be outgoing, but growing up I suppressed it, mostly around my dad. I chalk it up to patriarchal respect.

I'm not the person that raises her hand in class to answer a teacher's question. In fact, I hate it. I hate being put on the spot. That's the planner in me again. I like scripts. I love being on stage and performing for an audience, especially talent shows and plays. But improv? Forget about it.

For today, I brace myself. Clad in my cute outfit of jeans and top, I'm as armed and ready as I'll ever be.

It's 7 a.m., and I'm showered, dressed, and ready to go. We usually leave the house around 7:15 at the earliest. And that's only because I berate my mom and sister to get in the car so we can listen to Ryan Seacrest's *Ryan's Roses* segment. If you haven't guessed already, I'm also an early bird, and as my family would claim, impatient. Maybe a tad controlling. Jury's still out.

I really enjoy my morning routine, on most days. There's

something to routine in general I find very soothing. Predictable. Expected. There's traces of the planner again. I like waking up at the same time, in the same bed, in the same house. I've lived in this house since the day I was brought home from the hospital.

Textbook stability; no wonder I prefer consistency.

I wouldn't consider myself boring. An old soul, maybe. I can't wait until my age catches up with my soul. Maybe when I'm 30? Oy. That seems far away.

Downstairs, my dad is parked in his homestay. He doesn't leave his corner at the dining room table, which is perfectly positioned in front of the big screen TV until 1 p.m. at the earliest—when the markets close in Pacific Standard Time. Blue ink pen in hand, he meticulously maps his market analysis day by day, month by month, year by year. His cup of black tea—half nonfat milk with a teaspoon of sugar—sits atop a folded napkin to his left.

He has stacks of these charts dating back to the 80s, well before the conception of Samantha Selim. He shares stories of his first interest with the markets, while he was working for the conglomerate insurance company, John Hancock. He would spend his weekends at the pool of his apartment complex, charting the market trends as a hobby before it became his full-time gig.

I love that story. His biography is one for the books.

When I was a kid, I used to wake up at 6:09 a.m. (why this time, I'm not sure) and meet him in his home office (which is now my bedroom) for what you could describe as trivia.

It was basically math problems, equations, algebra—simple brain teasers, if you will.

Dad always wanted us to be the best in school. We, my siblings and I, always performed above the average.

I took it a step further and went beyond. I was usually the top grade in the class.

I don't really like the attention, but I like the recognition.

Is that hypocritical?

Now that high school is starting the pressure is on. College is coming up. I need to get into a good school and make it happen. I want my dad to be proud of me.

But first thing's first.

Today is the first day of the rest of my life.

So dramatic.

"Morning, Daddy," I chirp as I give him a hug and kiss.

He removes his eyeglasses and reciprocates with a kiss on the cheek.

"Hi Sammy, ready for school?"

"You know it."

And the conversation is over. There's not much more to say while the markets are in full swing.

I'm not offended. I've learned not to take it personally.

While the chatty being that I am craves conversation, I've taught myself to seek it elsewhere.

Cue my mama.

Jane is more than my mama. She's my best friend. We talk about everything under the sun, literally and metaphorically. She listens just as well as she gives advice. She shares just as well as she learns. She's funny without trying to be funny, especially when it comes to word pronunciations. Usually, given his later-in-life English language acquisition, my dad will mispronounce words like *Pythagorean* or *shrimps*. Mama takes it to a whole other level.

The other day, she was reading a *People* magazine article and asked me about "Odd-e-lay."

She was referring to Adele, the British pop star. I got a kick out of that one.

My favorite: she asked once about the drinking games kids play at parties.

"Bing bong?" she questioned.

"I think it's beer pong," I chuckled.

She's so unintentionally funny I cannot help but smile. Her Libra-ness balances my Aries-ness. Per the Zodiac, we make a great pair.

I don't know what I'd do without her.

She also has her teaching credential and initially taught pre-school and substituted before going into the *family business* of trading the markets. She's always loved and had a special connection with children; I can attest to this. The running joke amongst her colleagues always was how she worked at multiple forms of nurseries: plants and babies. Her nurturing nature cannot be questioned!

Let's not overlook her success in the markets. For ten years, she managed a commodity firm. The only woman in an industry full of men, she brokered many a deal and made a handsome sum of commissions in the process. She always said she was lucky because she never felt the glass ceiling, as the basis of her paycheck was based on sales, not corporate and societal politics that can riddle company dynamics and often dictate advancement. She worked in the markets until I was seven months old, when my sister was conceived and it became too difficult to manage accounts and her growing family at the same time.

My mom was married once before to a man named Jim, who she met via her high school boyfriend, Richard. Richard and Jim were best friends, and after Richard and Mom broke up, Jim sought Richard's permission to take out my mom.

Mama and Jim were married for eight years. They built their business together, a small firm in Orange County where she got her start trading commodities, until he was killed in a sky-diving accident. During his descent, he landed in an electrical fence and died there, tangled in the wiring. Mama was twenty-eight years old.

While I have grieved the loss of my mom's first mate, without this event, many things would not have happened, notwithstanding my own existence. Jim didn't want children. She wouldn't have met my dad, either, because she wouldn't have gotten into the markets.

Synchronicity is a wink from the universe.

Two people from opposite corners of the earth—India and North Dakota—met in California amidst the pursuit of their respective American dreams. My mom was the commodity manager. My dad was the client. That's a love story you can't make up.

Mama hasn't "worked" since I was born. She's managed all of our schedules, homework, sports, you name it. Dad has always worked out of the house, analyzing and making moves in the markets.

How lucky are we to have both parents at home.

There's that stability again.

Despite the undeniable safety I've been afforded throughout my upbringing, I also feel trapped. Overprotected. Kind of like the Britney Spears song.

I often suppress an innate need to explore, adventure, test the unknown. How else am I supposed to learn what's out there? How to handle the rough stuff?

I have insecurities. Exhibit A: I like recognition, but I hate attention.

But I'm also afraid of not being accepted. Good enough.

I blame the hormones. My estrogen levels are all over the place. I cry all the time. It's kind of exhausting.

Another thing to look forward to in adulthood. I hear these peaks and valleys level out eventually. Something called post-menopause.

In the meantime, I'm just trying to figure this life out.

Don't get me wrong. I am #blessed. But I am in pursuit of greatness. Like the Nike campaign, *Find Your Greatness.*

But first, day one.

We pull up to the curb at Balboa Bay High School, pool side, where the water polo team makes their residence. A litany of them are just making their way from the locker rooms to the heart of campus as I get out of the car. Their hair is still wet and their cheeks are still rosy from their morning workout.

What can I say? They're really hot.

I see Charlie walking through the gate and contemplate barking at her from down the sidewalk.

I refrain. I'm not interested in attracting any eyeballs.

So instead, I scamper as gracefully as possible after her, through the white iron gates and into the outdoor corridor that leads to the quad, where each clique has their designated hang-out spot.

Our spot, historically, has been a brick wall that acts as a planter for one of the palm trees on the north side, next to a statue of Triton, our mascot.

Whether that will change with our new "freshie" status remains to be seen. New year, new location, maybe?

"Charlieeeeeee," I purr as I get to what I think is within earshot of my tall blonde friend. She's a volleyball athlete and modelesque in stature. She'll be an All-American one day. This girl is already being recruited by the Ivy's and UCLA. I (playfully) hate her. One of my personal goals is to go to college on the East Coast, like Harvard or Columbia. Sometimes I wish I played a sport; I feel like it's a lot easier to get into school when you play a sport, or at least that's my perception.

Charlie was born Charlotte Christie Crichton, a name representing the capstone of alliteration. I too am proud of my alliterative name, Samantha Selim. I do not have a middle name. Daddy specifically omitted middle names for Sis and me, so that when we do get married our last name can become our middle name. (Honestly, I really like my name and have no intention of changing it, but we'll worry about that when it becomes a problem.)

Charlie is the third of five kids, and the only girl. It brings a whole new dimension to the term *middle child*. Her brothers, older and younger and ranging in age from ten to twenty (yes, her family had a busy decade in the bedroom) are protective but not overbearing. Her parents met on the real estate circuit, her mom an agent and her dad a developer. They were married for twenty years and divorced about five years ago. Her dad now lives in a condo on Oahu with his new wife, who's twenty-five. Her mom has a new husband, too, who has three kids from a previous marriage. They're all over eighteen and out of the house. These family dynamics lend to a fairly free-faring outlook for Charlie, whose blonde hair and blue eyes seemingly serve as a free pass for life.

She whips around and acknowledges my awkward greetings with that sly smile of hers. The *I know how uncomfortable you're feeling in this moment* smile. Love that about her.

"Hey girl, happy FDOS!"

"I'm leaping for joy."

She grins again.

"Where is your homeroom today?"

We only have homeroom on the first day of each semester, where the sole purpose is to get our class schedules. It's usually organized by last name.

I glance at the assignments posted on the side of the 200 building as I chased Charlie into the quad.

"I have Porter. You?"

"Dwyer," she announces as she rolls her eyes.

Charlie didn't like Mr. Dwyer since he caught her making out with who was now her ex-boyfriend in the AV room behind the gymnasium.

"So it will be a reunion," I teased.

At that moment Alex saunters up to us, parting the Red Sea by throwing her arms around both of our shoulders.

Alex has a flair for the dramatic. Alex Gladwell Norman, neé Alessandra, specializes in comedic relief. Sometimes I think it's a projection of her only-child-ness. She, too, is the product of divorce, one that was—from what I understand—increasingly nasty until the papers were signed. The irony that my two best friends in the world are progeny of family dissolution is not lost on me. The last time I checked, the divorce rate in America was right around sixty percent. Based on my own circle it seems to be going up rather than down. I've always thought I would get married, because I want a nuclear family like the one I was raised in. I'll worry about that when the choice becomes more relevant to my life.

Alex's mom was an actress; she's not super recognizable,

but one of those faces that showed up in a lot of ad campaigns and choruses over a substantial period of time. Her dad runs an ambulance company. When her mom retired from acting, she helped her then-husband out with balancing the checkbook and other operational tasks. Now, her mom collects alimony while her dad continues to support the family. I can't tell whether Alex is resentful of the family dynamics; if she is, she hides it with her humor. Which is a blend of Chris Rock, Baby Cobra, and Mindy Kaling—unexpected yet whimsical and dippy all at the same time. Her freckled cheeks and dirty blonde hair make her an approachable ally, resembling Rebecca from the American Girl doll collection.

"Hiiiiiiii girlssss."

Subtle.

"Sup, Alex," Charlie greets, somewhat facetiously.

"Working hard, or hardly working?" Alex retorts.

"Um, none of the above," responds Charlie.

"Aren't we feeling spritely today." Alex takes a step back and readjusts her Hershel backpack as her hair cascades around her shoulders.

"Who are you?" I judge. "James Bond?"

"I was going for Robert Pattinson, but close enough."

Oy.

"Alex, where is your homeroom?"

"Shepperd. She's new. Teaching biology this year, I believe."

"Fresh meat," Charlie muses.

She likes to challenge the teachers a bit—assess their bandwidth, if you will. She's sure to be voted "Most Likely to Start a Revolution."

The bell rings.

"Ladies, it's time," sounds Alex.

"You make it sound like we're about to walk the plank," Charlie balks, not amused.

"What a negative way to look at it!"

"Fine. Hurray. Woot woot. Better?"

"Tons."

"Okay girls," I interject. "See you at break."

"May you receive a fulfilling schedule with many hot boys," bids Alex.

"How very Yoda of you."

"What can I say? He's my hero."

CHAPTER THREE

WHAT IS TRUTH?

The day is a blur of hustle and bustle. I encounter classmates, old and new, in class and between classes. There's a subtle change in the way we present ourselves. As compared to the middle school days, I see the girls wearing extra layers of eye shadow and colored lip gloss. And higher hemlines. Tighter tank tops. You get the idea.

The guys look the same. Maybe their shoulders have better posture and stand a bit wider. Maybe.

I'm not sure how many different ways I can answer, "How was your summer?"

"It was good, how was yours?"

"It was good, too."

I feel myself getting dumber with this mind-numbing conversation. Granted I'm contributing to the dialogue, but still. Who really *cares* how my summer was?

For the record, we did a lot this summer, actually. My family and I took a three-week trip on a train across the entire country. For those who are claustrophobic, I wouldn't recommend it. However, no justice can be given to the variety of sights you can see in such a condensed period of time. Trailheading from LA's Union Station, we traversed the deserty Southwest, on through the bayous and basins of the South, turning north in Atlanta and up the everglade-laden Eastern Seaboard, and back again. We made multi-day stops in New York, Boston, Montreal, Toronto, Chicago—in that order.

Every city was different, a living tribute to its past, present, and future. They had similarities, of course: skyscrapers (glittering metallic reflections of the world above, around, and below), public transportation systems (mostly subways, some water taxis), and sports teams (we went to a Red Sox game at the oldest ballpark in baseball, Fenway Park)—yet each was uniquely positioned as a hub of growth, of potential.

Outside these cities, we saw the rural landscape, i.e. amber waves of grain, the majority of which quilts our country. Juxtaposed with our urban centers, sentinel sierras, and curated coastlines, it's an ironic illustration of our space that are these united, mostly contiguous, and utterly contrastive states. I digress.

I sit next to some new blood in my French class. He transferred from the Christian school in Santa Ana. He has a bookish charm to him—gilded Warby Parker frames paired with salmon-colored trousers and a Chambray button-down. Quite preppy. Almond skin tone and dark brown hair—in sum, a white boy with a nice tan. I don't catch his name.

After lunch we have drama, our elective class. Most freshmen take an elective this year to get it out of the way. Some choose painting; others, ceramics. I chose drama because, well, I like performing. We've been over this.

This is the one class that Alex, Charlie and I share on our schedule.

This could be fun.

Our entire class is made up of freshmen, except for one senior. The token misfit. His name is Ryan. He's hard to miss. He is the most vocal, I would say, of the class. Vocal as in, he won't shut up.

"Can someone share what you hope to learn in this class?" Ms. Lopez asks innocently.

This kid shoots his hand up like a pop-a-shot junkie.

"I see this class as a great opportunity to learn how to engage with people, not just on stage, but in everyday conversation. People can be really terrible communicators and I think we could learn a lot from you regarding how to not become one of those people and actually excel in this area."

Great. A soliloquist AND a kiss-ass.

"Why, thank you Ryan, for that response. Glad to see you're excited about this semester."

Ryan beams at her, then flickers his eyes over in my direction. He lingers his gaze a second too long, which makes me think I either have something on my face, or he's checking me out.

Truthfully, it's equally likely to be either.

Maybe it's just me, but his face looks somewhat confused, perplexed even. Like he's never seen a brown person before.

He's as white as snow. Albino, even.

Well, maybe not quite albino, but he's pretty fair. He has some freckles, likely from excessive sun exposure over the summer.

I try to smile and end up flinching a little.

Alex notices and gives me the *are you serious, what's wrong with you* look.

"Muscle spasm," I whisper.

The kid finally looks away and minds his own business. At least, for the rest of class. When the bell rings, Alex, Charlie, and I congregate by the door before parting ways for sixth period.

Sixth period is typically reserved for sports. Alex plays soccer, and Charlie, volleyball. I, on the other hand, am headed to science class—biology, specifically.

Fun, fun, fun.

My athletic requirements are fulfilled by during my fourth period dance class. I've never been much of a team sport athlete. I played community soccer for three years before retirement.

Let's not confuse my lack of interest in team sports with lack of interest in teamwork. There are critical differences, though some are not mutually exclusive.

"This day has felt SO long," Charlie pants.

"At least you guys are basically done today," I pine. "I still have one more to go." I hang my head in some degree of shame and defeat.

"Yeah, girl, I don't envy you. Who takes sixth period biology anyway?"

My eyes roll to the back of my head and stay there for a few minutes until she gets the memo.

"Okay, so, we're gonna go ..." Charlie leads with a nod towards the door.

"Fine. Leave me."

I'm so dramatic.

"Okay cool byeeeeee."

Such a teenager.

Fine, so I'm a little annoyed. Have some sympathy—or empathy?—I confuse the two sometimes.

I begrudgingly make my way around the corner of the 300 building towards the dimly lit back hallway that's home to most of the math and science classes at the school.

I don't mind it back here. The walls are lined with trophy cases, immortalizing victories by science fair winners and decathletes dating back to the founding of the school in 1962. It's a shrine to the smart people.

I actually really enjoy math and science. I'm pretty good at both, no bragging intended. Throughout middle school I consistently earned the highest grades on tests. Mid to high nineties about 95% of the time.

Do the math.

Ha.

When I get a ninety-seven on an exam, Daddy will say "what happened to the other three percent?"

Classic Indian response. Sometimes I wonder if my performance will ever be good enough. Good thing Mama is around to balance out his hard-ass-ness. Without her, my self-esteem would be doomed.

As I walk in, I see the usual suspects: the kids that forgo sports (like me), some girls that take fourth period dance with me, you get the idea.

I take a seat in the second row on the far side of the classroom. I hate when the first people into the classroom sit so close to the door. I'm not sure why. Maybe it's a coping mechanism, I don't know, it just bothers me. I hate a lopsided classroom.

Mr. O begins the last class of the day with the sixth welcome sermon every student has heard. A little creativity would be appreciated here.

Instead, as with all the others, he passes out the syllabus, which documents the next thirty-six-ish weeks in moderate detail. He combs through each line item, assignment, and deadline like a lab tech studies bacteria under a microscope.

The first time today was torture enough.

My neighbor seems to feel the same way, though she hides it better than me. The only indication is her recalcitrant body language: feet angled towards the door; shoulders ever so slightly slumped and oriented towards, again, the door; a smile plastered across her face so forced it's almost comical to look at.

In fact, I do laugh at it. It's more of a choke, to be honest. Fortunately, no one notices, as far as I can tell.

I've never seen this girl before. She looks older. I wonder what path of destiny led her to take this particular class, during this particular period.

I could ask her, I suppose. But I refrain. I don't want to appear judgmental.

Mr. O takes roll call. Her name is Kayla Howe; she prefers to be addressed as Kay.

I notice Kay drops a pencil beside her left foot, on my right. She doesn't appear to be aware of this travesty, so I pick it up for her.

"I think you dropped this," I whisper, laying the vintage No. 2 on the top left edge of her desk.

"Oh, thank you! I never would've noticed," she sings sweetly as if I just alerted her of an impending natural disaster. "What's your name?"

"I'm Samantha, I usually go by Sam or Sammy," I introduce myself meekly. "Are you new here?"

It turns out she's a senior who previously went to a high school where they offered Biology to seniors, not freshmen. Essentially a reversed science curriculum.

"And so," she continues, "here I am. What year are you?"

How flattering.

"I'm a freshman," I declare, I think for the first time out loud, ever.

"Wow, you look really mature for a freshman. I don't mean that in any sort of negative way, of course." I can feel her empathy in her words. It's refreshing; there's not much empathy floating around the freshman class, as far as I've seen.

"Maybe we can be study buddies?" She says. "I always find it helpful to have someone to compare notes with, if you're open to it."

I like her.

I'm not one to complain. But get me outta here.

As the pomp and circumstance of the first day of school finally draws to a close, I can feel the weight of the upcoming year make an impression on my heart muscle. And my right eyelid starts to twitch.

The 3 p.m. bell rings, and we are adjourned for the day. Praise Jesus. Or Allah. Or whoever brings you spiritual guidance.

I stop by my locker on the way to the parking lot. It's nestled up pretty close to the herb garden (I know, right) adjacent to the walkway that leads to my English class.

I offload my science book and continue on my way. I'm blocked by the mass exodus of middle schoolers and other high school folk who have a sixth period. The sea of students creates a bottleneck of traffic that I could really do without in this moment.

I don't like walking slow to begin with.

Deep breaths.

I see my mom parked at the edge of the lot by the tennis courts. Jenny, my sister, is already in the car.

As soon as I escape the bottleneck I dart towards the Lexus SUV, our family transport. I'm ready for this day to be over.

I keep my gaze on the ground ahead of me so as not to be sidetracked by passersby.

I'm not in the mood.

"Hi Samantha, how was your first day back?" Mama asks innocently in her sweet Midwest manner.

"Just peachy," I retort, probably unnecessarily. But I'm tired, so I figure it's justified.

We sit comfortably in silence for the drive home with no dialogue aside from the Top 40 hits on KISS FM. Yes. Peace.

Jenny doesn't talk much in general so that's not novel.

She generally keeps to herself. I admire that about her.

We pull up to the garage about twenty minutes later. Jenny and I jump out of the car before Mama parks. I grab a soda from the little refrigerator before heading inside, per my general routine.

Daddy has migrated to the couch opposite the big screen. It's covered in a blanket with photos of my siblings and me. We gave it to our parents as a gift for their twentieth wedding anniversary. His afternoons typically comprise of the daily news cycles and culminate with *Jeopardy!*, which we watch together. I will be on that gameshow one day.

"Hi Daddy," I greet him in the high-pitched voice that's literally reserved for him. He's the only one I alter my pitch for. Upon reflection, it's probably my attempt to be a kid in his eyes forever. Which will be true regardless of the pitch of my voice. Ah, yes, the psychology of it all.

"Did you learn anything today?" he chides. He thinks he's so funny. And he is, most of the time.

I quickly debate whether to play along or move on from the conversation. I choose the latter.

"No, not today."

Conversation terminated.

I pass through the dining room and turn the corner towards the stairs, making my way to my bedroom, my sanctuary. This space became my own a few years ago after Sis and I moved out of our shared room. We now share a Jack and Jill setup, and Bro moved into our room. My current room used to be Daddy's office. Jenny's room was a guest room / extra room.

My room has an animal print theme going on. It's like Mama says, trends always come back. Animal print, from what I understand was last popular in the 80s. Once or twice a generation seems to be the cycle.

I have leopard, tiger, zebra, cheetah (same as leopard?), you name it. They pair well with the all-black lacquered furniture and white walls.

This is in contrast to Jenny's room, which is more of an ode to the ocean.

We be opposites.

By the time I get to my room, which is in the back corner of the house above the garage, I'm dragging my feet with all the willpower I have left in me.

Suddenly I'm so tired.

I lazily toss my bookbag onto my makeshift couch-bed that's occupied by my colossal panda bear collection—which includes bears sized from keychain pets to a life-size edition. What can I say. They're so cute.

I keel over into my black (surprise) leather desk chair and laggardly log into my Gmail account.

I open my Gchat convo with Alex and Charlie. They've already engaged in an hour-or-so-long tirade since getting home at 2:30 p.m., per their free period.

It's mostly about their schedules and the new boys.

Charlie
did you see that one in math? he's flippin gorgeous  ima sucker for the light eyes and dark hair

"Girl, same," I think, but I don't type it.

Me
of course I saw him I ain't blind

Charlie
u ain't a hick either 😛

Me
that you're aware of 😏

Most times this is fun. But my mind is floating elsewhere.

It's drifting back to the blonde from drama class. He was really annoying. Kinda funny. Kinda obnoxious.

Clearly, he's made an impression.

I need some mind-numbing entertainment to take the edge off.

It's time to Netflix.

I change into my lululemon sweats and UCLA t-shirt before making my way back downstairs to the bonus room where we, in all honesty, spend most of our free time at home.

Jenny is already there, occupied by a plate of cheese and crackers. Yum.

My kryptonite.

I'm going to enjoy this. Who knows when I will have this level of peace again?

Every night before I go to sleep, I write in my journal. Sometimes, I'm so tired it takes the jaws of life to commit my oh-so-noteworthy (ha) thoughts to paper. I still use pen and paper, as opposed to my phone or laptop or other digitally-inclined device. There's something to how the brain muscle performs when writing by hand as compared to typing, something about the spatial relationship between the information captured, memory and literacy. Our brains truly weren't built to manage the capacity of information we are confronted with day in and day out. Today, it's something to the tune of 11 million stimuli *per day*. What a headache. What's more, I happen to like the feeling of my uni-ball pen on my leathery-textured paper. It's part of the experience, I think. I digress.

Sometimes I write about my day, recounting the highlights and lowlights all the same. Most times, though, I write about my truth.

What is truth?

Socrates, our friend from history class, defines truth as "a wandering that is divine." I've always been intrigued by philosophy, mostly because I don't understand it. It's making it my own that's the fun part.

Wandering implies a journey, a search, an aimless pursuit lacking intention. Socrates describes truth as a journey with intention, guided by God or godlike intervention. While I cannot speak for Socrates, for my own relationship with God is tenuous as best, he would probably view truth as what we today term soul searching. The questions become … What are you looking for? What is your truth?

To help me explore this part of myself, I use a three-step prompt. It's straightforward and simple to answer, on most days.

First is acknowledging the raw awareness of the unspoken "I am." Sometimes we call these affirmations. I am strong. I am determined. I am unafraid—you get the idea. Writing affirmations suggests a connection to potential, to the future, to hope.

Secondly, I write down what I'm grateful for. Practicing gratitude means paying attention to what we are thankful for and appreciate, like hot coffee, morning beach runs, and friends to call late at night with a crisis.

Finally, I write what I'm looking forward to, whether it's the weekend, my next yoga class, or brunch on Sunday.

Today, my entry looks like this:

I am …
    Hopeful for a new school year full of promise
    Open to possibilities
    Embracing opportunities in my space
    Not holding onto the past and focusing on what I can

control
Grateful for...
  My spunky friends
  Cute boys
  Cheese plates
  Nights at home, the walls and people that built me
  The waves crashing outside, the consistency and peace
  it brings
Looking forward to ...
  Learning more about Blondie
  My next yoga class
  Breakfast
  Seeing what this year brings

I find this exercise not only therapeutic, but also an exercise in consistency. Being the old soul / academic scholar that I am, I've learned about what studies call the consistency principle: people are inherently motivated toward cognitive consistency and will change their attitudes, beliefs, perceptions, and actions to achieve it. This guy named Robert Cialdini and his research team have conducted extensive research into what Cialdini refers to as the *Consistency Principle of Persuasion*. It's similar to the idea of habit, creating routine, and the discipline that enables these behaviors.

I personally enjoy consistency, and seem to have benefited from its effects, like those 6:09 morning math sessions with Daddy and evening *Jeopardy!* viewing parties, the routine synonymous with our family dynamics.

My thoughts still wander, though the discipline helps me reel them back in. I'm by no means perfect at it. But I practice. And what's that they say—practice makes perfect? I guess that depends on your definition of perfection, which is another rabbit hole entirely.

But for now, I sleep.

CHAPTER FOUR
BLONDIE

Another dawn, another day.

The early riser that I am, I wake up with the sun. Often before my alarm rings. It's a blessing and a curse.

The second day of school is typically more content-driven than the first, which feels more like social hour times seven. While I'm into social hour, I also like going to school for school's sake. Let's get into it.

My daily routine is, you know, routine. By the time lunchtime rolls around, I'm feverish for the day to be over.

But first, drama class.

Irony: the first person I see when I walk is, you guessed it, Blondie. My luck.

He's sitting directly opposite me on the far side of the room. We make eye contact. He smiles, somewhat sheepishly. He casts his eyes from mine to his hands, which are studiously folded on the desk in front of him.

Teacher's pet, is my first thought.

I disengage my gaze and take a seat in front of the entrance, in direct conflict with my pet peeve.

Fine, I'm a hypo.

As luck (?) would have it, he actually GETS UP to come over and speak to me.

I'm not prepared for this.

"Hi."

"Hey."

"This might come off a bit creepy, but do you live near eleventh street by any chance?"

Wait, what?

"Who's asking?" is the first response that comes to my mind, but I recover quickly, though not exactly gracefully.

"It's a possibility. Do you spend a lot of time on the peninsula?" Somewhat accusatory in tone, but I think it gets the point across.

"Actually, I do."

Oh. Cool.

"Yeah, I'm a City Lifeguard and I worked at Tower 11 on Monday's this summer. I thought I recognized you. You were wearing a black bikini with bedazzled accents, right?"

Holy hell. That's rich. It takes a brave man to say *bedazzled* out loud.

My face apparently betrays my thoughts. He looks at me a tad perplexed.

"I'm starting to think you think that's creepy," he hesitates.

I chuckle a bit. "I mean, wouldn't you?"

He pauses.

"Yes, but I'd also be flattered."

Shots fired.

"I didn't say I wasn't flattered."

"No, but your face did."

Touché.

His tone is playful, of the witty banter variety that I enjoy so much.

I'm in trouble.

"Well, rest assured I'm sufficiently flattered."

"Good. My work here is done."

And with that, he returns to his claimed seat at the opposite side of the room. By the time our exchange ends, three quarters of the classroom is full.

I shift my body back and forth in my chair in an attempt to regain my composure. I notice Alex and Charlie snuck in during our verbal spar.

Their faces betray their thoughts, too. Alex's smirk is wider than a Mack truck. I sense a theme.

"So," snips Charlie, somewhat accusatory in nature. Typical. "What was that about?"

"You're gonna love this," I lead. "You remember the lifeguard from Monday?"

"Hmm-hmm."

I turn my head and linger a gaze in Blondie's direction for dramatic effect.

"Shut up."

"I didn't say anything," I reply facetiously.

It's Charlie's turn to trade a look.

"Damn Sam, he's pretty cute. And a *senior*." Emphasis added.

"Finally, someone who's maturity is somewhat on par with mine."

"Girl, you're an old soul. You'd need to date a college guy if maturity is what you're after. And you're fourteen. That's gross."

Point taken.

"Plus, your dad would probably have a heart attack."

She's not lying.

"Okay okay, are we done yet? Class is about to start."

"Not even close, but I'll give you a pass," Alex chides.

Like it's some kind of favor. Thanks, girl.

Meanwhile, I catch Blondie—or Ryan, his given name—snickering to himself, apparently observing our girl talk.

I shoot him a glare—wrinkled nose, furrowed brow, the works—which he returns with a similar contortion of his face. Followed by a smile, and oof, a wink.

Oh Jeez, this could be fun. Again, I'm in trouble.

Throughout this class I catch myself looking for any excuse to look in his direction. I might be imagining things, but I *think* he's doing the same. At least, he is in my mind.

I'm not even sure what the lesson was. My thoughts were occupied by visions of his guardy-ness wrapped in a beach towel and sitting on the edge of Tower 11, his feet dangling, his upper body accepting the kiss of the sun's rays.

Is this healthy?

Good thing I'm a good multitasker. People say studies show it's impossible to multitask because the brain can process too many sequences at once, or something like that.

Whatever the reasoning is, I'm sure I can manage. I think. I hope.

The dismissal bell snaps me back to reality. I move at a glacial pace, somewhat intentionally, to see what Ryan's move is going to be.

I avoid direct eye contact, but in my periphery I can make out his movement. I sense him moving, slowly in the mass of classmates, towards the door.

Just as he passes the row of desks where I'm sitting, our eyes meet.

"See you tomorrow, Sam," he says with one of those nods surfer boys use to communicate.

"See you," I manage. I have a pang in my stomach. Shortness of breath. God, I hate hormones.

I attempt to shun the wave of rejection that washes over me. I don't even know what I wanted to happen. But it sure as hell wasn't that.

I'm going to stew on that missed opportunity for all of sixth period.

After school we make our annual trip to STAPLES, for none other than school supplies. Usually, each teacher provides a list of necessary items required for their class. Syncing these four or five lists can be a somewhat daunting task. There's got to be an app for that, other than the obvious Amazon. Most times each list includes a binder, set of dividers, pens and/or pencils (depending on the subject), a red pen for correcting, a highlighter for emphasis. For math we're usually expected to have a compass, a protractor, a ruler of some kind. Besides science, it's probably the most high-maintenance class with, ironically, the most minimal output. English essays are much more intensive than math computation, as far as I'm concerned.

I'm still wallowing, somewhat wistfully, about my encounter with Ryan. I try to put a pin in it for the next hour or so as we wade through the seemingly hundreds of primary and secondary school-aged folk with their tandem guardians, who decided that the second day of school was a better day to attempt the school supply showdown (as compared to the first day).

We, my mom and sibs and I, have done both, and honestly the intensity is about the same. The inventory seems to be better on day two.

We go to the STAPLES on 17th Street, which is central to Newport Cove High School, not BBHS. When I was in sixth grade, my parents transferred me to Eastcliff, a brand-new elementary school that feeds into BBHS. The thought was that BBHS followed a more academically-inclined curriculum, offering more AP classes and opportunities for a more advanced education—a very Indian approach to schooling, it seems. I had gone to the same school since kindergarten, and so when I left Balport Elementary, I also left over half a decade's worth of friendships. Fortunately I met Alex and Charlie at Eastcliff, and all was forgiven.

Days like today are nostalgic, because we see a lot of the kids I used to go to school or play soccer with. Soccer teams were also formed along city lines. I played for three seasons before completely dedicating myself to my yoga practice. For whatever reason, I'm just not a team-sport-kind-of-girl. I think it's more of a reflection of my aerobic athleticism than my ability to work in a team.

Casually, I see Marla, our star forward from our U-15 team

last season. We happened to win the city championship that year. What a fluke, that was. It doesn't detract from her uncanny ability to execute a give-and-go comparable to the likes of Alex Morgan. She'll play professionally one day. It makes me think about one of those ironies of life: MVP-caliber athletes can play years without a championship; I happened to win one during my third year in AYSO soccer and I'm not even that good. The parallel may be a little dim, but it just goes to show that being the best doesn't get you everywhere, and, most notably, timing is everything.

I offer Marla a passing wave as I return my attention to choosing my personal pencil pouch for the next 178 school days. Priorities.

As I identify my new pencil pouch—a delicate pink with gold filigree—I venture to find Mama and company, presumably looking at the assortment of pee-chee folders that sport vintagey athletes.

On my way through Aisle Six, which houses the desk calendars and day planners, I catch a glimpse of Shane Pearson. Shane is someone I knew throughout all of grade school. An athletic kid, he always scored the most during Capture the Flag and two-hand-touch. He always wore these RVCA shirts, the clothing brand his dad worked for. He must've gotten his growth spurt, because we used to be the same height. Now Shane's close to six feet. Again, those hormones.

I always had a crush on him, but I never verbalized it. I never verbalize crushes in any capacity. Aside from that one time last year, when I told my guy friend Adam that I liked his friend James—the defining experience that inspired the rule.

James is the All-American athlete, plays a sport for every season (football, basketball, baseball), and also performs well academically. He won Scholar Athlete of the Year for our class last year. Adam is smart, too. He plays football, defensive end I think.

He has a funny, ha-ha sense of humor, versus a funny, witty one, like James. I'm not sure if Adam was mad at me, or maybe jealous of James? In any event, Adam ended up betraying my secret to James *himself*. James and I were friends before that. We'd talk in class, compare notes, talk about sports. I'm actually fairly well-versed in sports.

Not only does my brother play, but as a family we spend a lot of time together watching everything from football to baseball to basketball—not so much hockey, for whatever reason. It compliments our *Jeopardy!* viewership nicely; a little bit brawn, a little bit brain. Sports is one of those universal languages, the rawest form of human grit, passion, and strength there is, that transcends all boundaries, real or imagined. While Daddy grew up playing *kabaddi* and *cricket*, and yes, *futbol*, we grew up watching multi-billion-dollar leagues that give athletes the platform to become superstars. While the contrasts are great, each game is a distinctly human creation, as unique to humanity as is consciousness. A literal leveling of the playing field, pun intended. Plus, it's something fun and entertaining to indulge in together, like a story, a narrative contextualized by players, plot twists, and PR-performances.

I digress.

After Adam's letdown, you could clearly sense a shift in James's behavior towards me. Adam's duplicity took place during finals week. While emotionally frenzied and embarrassed, I still pulled off my straight As (as if there was any doubt). Thankfully, summer acted as a shock absorber, for both him and I, I'm sure. Now I just pretend nothing happened and avoid both of them, circumstances permitting. Call it an act of self-preservation.

Shane sees me and acknowledges my presence amidst the chaos that comes with shopping for school supplies. We exchange *hey*'s and continue on our own ways. It's really true; men speak notably less words per day than women.

I find my crew and make sure I have everything I need so that I don't lose points for not having the right kind of highlighter. One time, in elementary school, my teacher said that if we didn't bring in the *exact* highlighter that she showed us as an example, we wouldn't get credit and would miss recess the next day. I'm not even sure if that's allowed; there's only so much one can control about such things. Not to mention, do you know how many brands and types of bulky, yellow highlighters there are in the world? To send a child on that kind of scavenger hunt who at the end of the day has zero purchasing power is ridiculous.

We manage to get out of there by 4:30 p.m. My mind instantly goes back to Ryan and the less-than-eventful interaction we shared at the end of drama class.

When I get home, I go straight to Gchat to wallow and share my defeat with Alex and Charlie.

They're supportive of my disappointment.

Charlie
bottom line, he's a boy. Boys are idiots

Alex
Yeah true. doesn't make it any less
annoying

Me
right

Charlie
I wonder if he has a girlfriend?? 🤔

Alex
def a possibility. thats something we
could easily find out. @Charlie?

Charlie
way ahead of you. sources tell me he
was dating a sophomore. broke up
before summer. it was mutual. aside
from her, word on the street is he hasn't
dated much

Charlie has a direct line to GG—Gossip Gabs. On occasions like these, I'm grateful for that.

Alex
maybe he's gay?

The catch-all rationale for lack of interest.

Me
call me crazy but I doubt it.

Charlie
maybe you were giving fuck off vibes?

I pause and ponder. Could that be it?

Alex
yah sammsies, sometimes you can be a
lil intimidating. like your big words and
stuff. maybe it scared him off..

Great. Me and my big bad words.

Me
so you're saying I should change myself
just so I can get attention from a boy!?

Charlie
ding, ding, ding 🔔 🔔 🔔 we have a
winnaaaaaaaa

Me
sounds like alotta work

Alex
do you want the guy or not?

Me
honestly, im not sure anymore

Alex
porqui?

Me
It feels fake.and if I feel shitty now
what will I feel like if I chase him and he
rejects me? I'm just not sure if it's worth
the effort. I'm not even allowed to date!!

Charlie
sounds like you're scared

Me
no shit, sherlock.

Alex
sounds to me like you've got two
choices. you can live in fear..fear of
rejection. OR you can live with hope..
hope that what's meant to be will be

Charlie
that was deep

Me
that's nice Alex, but neither option gives
me much control

Alex
as much as you'd like to Samantha
Dearest you can't control everything

Me
I can try

Alex
Good luck with that

I know they're just trying to help.

Me
The real question is do I really want to
pursue this guy? I mean, he's a senior.
can you imagine how much crap I'll get
from people?! he's probs not a virgin.
That's like a whole other level of stress

I'm not ready to have sex. I've thought about it, been to health
classes, yadda yadda. Truthfully I'm pretty closed minded to the

whole thing.

Charlie
sounds like you're confusing stress with
hot sex

Charlie and her two cents.

Me
at this point they're one and the same
to me

And that's the God honest truth.

Alex
u have a lot to think about Sam. But
don't think too hard. it takes the fun out
of it

I guess that depends on what you define as fun.

Me
sound advice thanks gals

It's 10 p.m. already. Sleepy time.

Me
Im gonna crash. chat ya later xo

I doubt I'll sleep tonight. Lots to think about. Over and out.

CHAPTER FIVE
JUST BREATHE

The next day I feel haggard and so not cute. I didn't sleep great, per my prediction. Self-fulfilling prophecy? Perhaps.

In any case, I'm in no mood for B.S. Which is generally true, but especially today.

By the time fifth period rolls around, my energy levels are like that of a sloth. However, I make a concerted effort to avoid Ryan—see how he likes being ignored.

Funny story, he's not even in class today. Hooray.

But also, ahhhhhh!!!! He's not even around for me to avoid. WTF.

Just breathe.

Upside: I'm not in my best form and probably would've said something stupid anyway.

Yeah. This is good. I can let my guard down.

I get through class relatively unscathed. The teacher called on me once—I hate when they do that—and I manage to produce a somewhat eloquent response despite my melodramatic state.

The question was something about screenplays and the different parts of a story: setting, climax, denouement, etc. …

The only reason I know a thing or two about it is from my seventh grade drama class where most of the content of the class consisted of quizzes based on stuff we talked about. It's kinda hard to explain why it was effective. I remember really enjoying it.

Clearly it paid off in this moment.

Once class is over, I again, like clockwork, make my way over to Bio.

As I turn the corner down the hallway, lo and behold, Ryan is casually standing outside my classroom.

I feel my stomach contract and my breath shorten.

"Are you stalking me now?" I hear myself say as I approach him.

"Maybe. Would that be an acceptable form of flattery?"

Boy, this kid is good.

"Depends. What's the purpose?"

He smiles coyly as he glances at the ground between us before returning his gaze to mine.

"Well, I'd like to ask you on a date."

Oh shit. I'm not ready for this.

"Is that so? Is this you asking, or are you trying to gauge whether I will say yes depending on my current vibes?"

He smiles and chuckles again. "I'm not sure, but I think it's the latter?"

This is fun.

"Are you asking me or telling me?"

"It's a qualified tell."

"Okay, that's vague."

"Tell can have a negative connotation. Hence the qualified part. Asking in this instance I think implies a lack of assertiveness. Which, as I've gathered from our interactions, you may consider to be a weakness. Does that sound about right?"

"My answer is a qualified maybe."

This time he lets out a guttural laugh, one which elicits the attention of fellow students.

He looks around and turns a deep shade of sunburn, but recovers nicely and resumes our conversation.

"In that case, I'd like to ask you to dinner on Saturday night. Would you be interested?"

I am, quite honestly, but something inside me hesitates. There's frankly a whole lot of somethings.

My dad, for one. No chance he'd let me hang out with a boy. Alone.

People will talk. Nothing says gossip like a senior boy dating a freshman girl.

He seems nice enough.

All of this is going through my mind as he's standing in front of me, waiting for my response.

I think the silence finally gets to him, as he says, "No pressure. Why don't you think about it and get back to me?"

He hands me a folded sheet of paper, presumably with his phone number on it.

"Okay," I muster. "I'll think about it."

Oy. Was not expecting that.

Now I actually have a decision to make. It's no longer theoretical, but a reality I get to deal with.

You know the saying, *don't worry about it until it becomes a problem?*

Well, this is definitely a problem.

It's funny how dire and shunned one can feel in one moment—and how in the next, it's a completely different ballgame.

Let's face it. It's self-imposed. And yet, we continue to behave this way. There's gotta be some science to that.

Perceptions are basically a mindset. Like awkwardness. Fear. Hope.

How do I change my mindset?

Story of my young life.

The rest of my day is riddled with thoughts around Ryan, this exchange, this theoretical date, the pending onslaught of potential gossip.

Gossip. Every high school's currency. Do I really want to be the subject of dating drama for the student body?

No. Hell no.

Am I overthinking it?

Probably. But that doesn't make the reality any less difficult to navigate.

My head hurts. When I get home, I grab a soda and pop some ibuprofen, intent on numbing the pounding in my temples. I don't usually like taking pills, but today I make an exception. The only other time I make an exception is during my period.

Even school doesn't pain me this much.

I immediately Gchat Alex and Charlie to regale them with this latest turn of events.

Alex
so you're gonna go right?!?!?

Me
I dunno

Charlie
whats to know???

Me
im nervous about what everyone will
say. I don't want that kind of attention

Charlie
Sam, that is a terrible reason

Alex
no I think it's a good reason.

Me
oh?

Alex
being a kid at that school is hard
enough. why would you purposefully
make it harder on yourself

Charlie
when did you get so insightful?

Alex

comes in waves

Ain't that the truth.

She has a point, though. Why would I purposefully make it harder on myself?

Only when it's worth it.

Is it worth it?

Part of me feels an obligation to be a good Indian daughter and avoid this scenario entirely.

Part of me says "F that, live a little."

The remaining part of me asks, "People are going to talk, can you handle it?"

That's a lot of competing thoughts for one night, let alone one 14-year-old. When did life get so complicated?

The biological answer is driven by hormones. The social answer is when we made it so.

As I lay in bed, my mind swims upstream, embroiled by currents that epitomize my contrarian thoughts. My breath shortens again.

Finally, around 11 p.m., I fall asleep. It wasn't a good sleep, but sleep nonetheless. I have my answer.

It's fifth period, and Ryan approaches me the second we notice each other's presence.

"I can't, I'm sorry." No context. No lead in. God, I can be a bitch sometimes.

His reaction is less than rattled.

"No worries. We'll find another time."

Clearly he's not getting the message.

Before I can respond, he walks away with that goofy grin of his smacked across his face.

What a weirdo. Good thing I said no. Dodged a bullet there.

Or so I thought.

CHAPTER SIX
CHOICES

When I feel scattered and uncentered, yoga is my escape. It might sound kooky to come. It sounded kooky to me before I first tried it. It took me a few months of classes to even begin to reap the benefits of the practice.

Now I'd consider myself a regular.

There's something about the calm, the connection to breath that soothes me. It's the synergetic yet disparate roles of the mind and body. Yoga helps me get out of my head and into my body. I can focus on building strength in my physical being, and train my mind not to talk me out of it.

My teacher, Jett, holds a guru-like place in my life. Put simply, a guru is a spiritual guide, a teacher, a mirror who reflects one's personal potentials of existence. Jett has practiced yoga for a long time, practicing well over five decades of mantras and meditation. She grew up as a dancer in New York, became a Rockette at the age of fifteen, and performed alongside the likes of Barbara Streisand

and Bob Fosse for years before retiring to—practice yoga. She found solace, she says, from an industry that, while empowering and entertaining, at times leaves its participants extinguished and lacking existence. Jett turned to yoga as a resource for reinvigoration, a restitution of her spirit and selfish act of self-love. Her stories of rigmarole backstage and in rehearsal, not to mention her travels, should be documented. I hope she writes a book one day. For now, she plays the role of my maternal yogic master.

One Saturday, my mom was busy running around taking my brother and sister to their soccer games. Saturdays are challenging to coordinate these days, especially when there are three kids with three schedules and two parents/chauffeurs to make it all happen. I had yoga at 11 a.m. and my dad was supposed to take me. At 10:45 a.m., I came downstairs, yoga mat and water bottle in tow, and asked Daddy if he was ready to go.

I'm not sure if it was the tone of my voice, but for whatever reason, he erupted with a *don't tell me what to do*-toned response (I don't remember the exact verbiage due to my shock), to which I fled the scene and went to my room to cry.

About twenty minutes later, he came into my room and said, nonchalantly, that he would take me now.

By then, the class had already started and Jett has a rule about tardiness. I don't like to break the rules.

But we went, and I entered the studio wearing a tear-stained expression and shaking from the past and present failure I'd apparently been bringing to the adults. From her perch next to her control panel for the music and lights, Jett looked at me with a mien of maternal disappointment, before realizing the stress on my face.

And I just start bawling, in front of all the students.

"My dad...got mad at me..." I managed to blurt between sobs.

Jett threw her arms around me so I could bury my face in her shoulder and release my pangs of guilt, fear, and failure. She led me to the sitting room where she displays her costumes of performances past, which also serves as her lounge and bedroom. Not only does she conduct her classes here, she also *lives* here, a true testament to her commitment to her art.

"There, there," she consoled. "It'll pass."

And then, she whispered, in her hauntingly harmonious voice, "Remember, Samantha, dear child: you are the sky, everything else is just the weather."

This is one of my favorite mantras I learned from Jett.

And she was right. When Daddy picked me up forty-five minutes later, all was forgiven. He and I have that kind of relationship in any case; I just don't like disappointing him. In the end I can't control these things, and so, I move forward. Jett taught me that. Yoga taught me that.

Yoga has captured the hearts, minds, and bodies of many a spirit. It's now all but a mutually agreed upon method to increase flexibility, gain strength, and reduce stress. What's more, it's also a 5000-year-old system of mental and physical practices which includes philosophy, meditation, breathing exercises, lifestyle and behavior principles, and physical exercise. Not to mention, it originated in India, a happy coincidence given my birthright.

Like my own young life, yoga's history is vast and complex, with bountiful constructs of texts, teachers, and traditions, that compare and contrast with one another. The practices we experience today are a synthesis of philosophies over thousands of years.

Not to make this a lesson on the history of yoga, but the six main variations of yoga in Hindu philosophy are raja, karma, jnana, bhakti, tantra, and hatha. Though the ultimate goals may vary, each style requires self-inquiry and certain disciplines to reach the desired state. One translation of the word "yoga" is "union"—thus, the practices seek to bring union in some form or another: body, mind, and spirit; earthly and divine; even oneness with all.

The physical practice of yoga—hatha yoga—is the most predominant form in the West today, although it really only developed into its current form over the last 200 years. The goal of hatha yoga is to balance the mind, body, and spirit through physical practice, breath work, and meditation.

While I applaud the accessibility of yoga practice today— the prevalence of private studios and lululemon is astoundingly overwhelming to quantify—there's a certain commercialization that capitalism brings to any product or service when it reaches such a pinnacle of pervasiveness. Yoga is no exception to this rule.

Is that a good reason to stop practicing? Of course not.

It's too valuable an asset to my peace to omit.

My peace, I describe, is the awareness and acceptance of my being. Who I am, what I want, where I'm going. My peace includes the varying dimensions that comprise the self: mind, body, spirit, and the connective layers in between. Sometimes these layers disaggregate, leaving personal thoughts, feelings, and vessels scattered and unattuned to what the self needs.

Yoga's roots are embedded in the union of these concepts. Early Sanskrit texts such as the Vedas (1500 BCE) and the Upanishads (500 BCE) explain and explore yoga as a means of access to the Divine and a way to connect the earthly form with the spiritual form. The Vedas tell stories of the Hindu gods while referencing yoga techniques in Vedic rituals. The Upanishads, which focus on philosophy, contain the first documented use of the term "yoga," where it refers to a firm holding back of the senses to join with the supreme state of being.

Note that there is no mention of physical practice in these

texts—only philosophy, worship, and meditation.

On the heels of the Upanishads came the Bhagavad Gita in 200 BCE, the Hindu story of moral dilemma which underscored the importance of meditation to overcome suffering.

And in 150 BCE, the sage Patanjali published what we know as the Yoga Sutras, a collection of aphorisms guiding the lifestyle and habits of those seeking to attain wisdom through yoga. The sutras describe the personal power and liberation available through yoga, and include rules regarding prayer and worship, eating, breathing, attitudes, thoughts, meditation, and even sexual relations.

There's something of value for everyone.

For me, the value is in acknowledging my thoughts and the power I assign to them.

How often do I allow my thoughts to talk me out of something?

Too often, that's the answer.

I've noticed a majority of the time it's out of fear, out of believing the worst-case scenario will be my reality, as opposed to hoping for the best.

It's the duality of hope and fear.

Sometimes, especially in today's world, we wear masks to protect ourselves from external forces that may harm us. The teenage years are a great example. Here I am wrestling a quandary that, at this point, only exists in my mind. These forces may manifest in forms of danger, or fear—real or perceived. Call it self-preservation.

Sometimes, our masks become our behavior so much so that they become our identity. This is where awareness becomes important. This self-deception inevitably disconnects us from our truth we concurrently seek. How do we get past this manifestation of fear?

This is why I write in my journal each night. Not only is it an escape, a lamenting of sorts, but an opportunity to explore and express my truth. Speaking truth is an act of self-inquiry, of introspection. From this self-inquiry, we find peace in our truth. Is it uncomfortable? I compare it to getting the flu: there are pointed moments of displeasure, sometimes pain, but eventually it goes away and I move on. At least that's what my yoga teacher says.

I feel fear and shame.

In my class this Saturday, I try to skew my thoughts towards hope rather than fear, consciously and with intention.

My word of intention for this class is strength. How do I find the strength to embrace this new situation and explore the opportunities associated with it? How do I tap into my inner beast mode and use that to power my actions?

Again, so much of it is a mental game. The more you practice and engage, the more routine and seemingly natural it feels.

How do I apply this approach to Ryan?

First off, I need to figure out what it is that I want. Do I want to get to know him at all? Depending on the answer, beyond that I need to make choices that support the answer.

Consistency at its finest.

Closing class with an exhaustive breath of *namaste*, I have a better understanding of what it is I want.

I want to exercise my power of choice.

Choices require space—both internally and externally. Clutter can inhibit this process, I find. To absolve myself of this problem, I walk out to the sand and just sit. This is especially helpful in the fall months, when the weather is nice but there's no one around—our Indian Summer. Creating this external space allows for clearing of internal space, particularly in the mind, with a focus on breath.

I want to discover.

I want to be a little dangerous and live at the edge of my comfort zone.

In the end, my obligation to myself is to soften through the fear. Choices, big and small, can have drastic effects on the psyche, but the key is to not allow that fear to plant seeds and grow.

Who wants to be unhappy with the choices that we make in this life? Sometimes, though, we do make decisions where the outcome is less than subpar, and we just have to live with it.

I accept these realities and my current exploration—no matter how inconsequential it may seem to the casual observer. All we can do is put in the effort.

Perhaps I should meditate on it more.

CHAPTER SEVEN
THEY KNOW

It's Monday again. After a somewhat therapeutic weekend—yoga, beach (the weather is still beautiful), and helping Mama tend her roses—I'm ripe with a renewed energy, like the Energizer Bunny got a new battery pack and a set of drums.

Mama is the quintessential caretaker and a nurturer by nature. She tended plant nurseries for Sears during her high school days, and sold more lawnmowers than her commissioned counterparts. I've never fully figured this out, since she's more of an introvert than extrovert. Not that introverts can't successfully sell, the data simply implicates it is statistically less likely.

Today she sustains her green thumb by maintaining her roses and plumerias at home. She has about twenty-five different varieties of each, accompanied by other plants such as sago palms, strings of pearls, rabbit tracks, donkey tails, all sorts of philodendrons, chefloras, and more. Mama diligently waters each plant according to their thirst, coordinated via a timed sprinkler system. She pots and re-pots the flowers when they outgrow their homes, and ensures that their access to the sun is consistent with their daily needs. I don't know how she keeps them all straight; it's a lot to manage, but she does it well and does it with flare. Plus, a surplus of oxygen never hurt anyone.

In addition to her plants, Mama is also a collector of books, candles, Buddha statuettes, and assorted nutcrackers—not to mention various holiday decor. Our home is always festive and full of color, a cathedral devoted to the appreciation we have for this life we share together.

Today, my game face is on. This expression mostly looks like my normal face—calm, happy, pleasant—but with a glimmer of fire behind my hazelly-green eyes. (Green eyes are considered a rarity and thus a mark of beauty amongst Indian people.) It's subtle but notably fierce.

At least, I think so. I can feel it in the adjusted alignment of my vertebrae when I walk. In the stretched arches of my feet. In the ligaments where my neck and shoulders meet.

Let's go Monday.

Clearly my chakra is palpable. First thing, Ryan sees me from across the quad and beelines to the lockers where I'm standing, radiating good vibes.

"Someone looks like they had a nice weekend," he surmises.

"I did enjoy myself," I share. "How about you?"

"It was decent. Tried to get in some time in the water, but the waves were a little choppy for my taste."

Surfer slang for "the waves sucked."

"Tough break. Pun intended." I'm so funny.

Ryan lets out a guttural laugh. Authentic. Hmm.

"I try."

I'm so proud of myself.

"Have you given any thought to my proposal?"

"What, are we getting married, or something?"

Sunburn doesn't even begin to describe the shade of red his face turns.

"I'm just busting your balls."

I pause.

"Actually, yes, I have."

"Yes? Is that your answer?"

"As a matter of fact, it is. Though that 'yes' was specific to your first question. But what the hell, take it as a yes to both."

"I'm not going to try and backpedal through that thread of logic and just enjoy the 'yes' for what it is. How does this weekend work for you?"

"I'll have to check my schedule, but Saturday should work fine."

I'm free as a bird, but he doesn't need to know that.

"Great, it's a date." He winks at me.

I'm consumed by a combined feeling of creeped out and surprise.

Is he one of those PDA people?

Guess we'll find out.

By fifth period, the rumor mill is churning gossip like it's going out of style.

Walking into drama class, thankfully flanked by Alex and

Charlie, the whispers are all too conspicuous to ignore.

They know.

It's only been a few hours!

My naïveté never fails to surprise me.

"Sam," Quinton, a fellow freshie, unapologetically barks at me, "Are you and Ryan dating?"

Super tactful, Quinton.

"Where did you hear that?" I counter, trying not to sound defensive.

"Honestly, I'm not sure. It's a hot topic today though, that's for sure."

Nice.

I avoid answering his pointed question and look to Alex and Charlie for moral support.

During break and lunch, we gab about my new prospect and all the intrigue surrounding the situation. So many layers, yet simple at the same time.

My girls are uber supportive. Plus, they're familiar with my antics. Which can be a blessing or a curse, depending on what side of the fence you're on.

"He totally wants you," Alex, ever the shy one, proclaims.

"I concur," chimes Charlie. "Very few guys would risk rejection twice. It's just not the way they're built."

"Thank you for the biology lesson, Charlie," I quip. "I feel smarter already."

"I wonder where he's going to take you," muses Alex.

"Let's be real. He's not going to *take* me anywhere. My mother will be doing that."

I'm presuming at this point that she'll be okay with this pseudo-date situation and help me find a way to go without my dad being all weird and protective.

We'll worry about that later.

"You know what I mean." This time I get the eye roll. Subtle.

"In any case, it will be my first real date. So let's not try to make it more hyped than it needs to be."

I make eye contact with them.

"Please."

Wishful thinking.

As if fifth period was any indication.

I feel eyeballs darting in my direction from every which way, like I'm some kind of exhibit at a social ecology museum.

Including Ryan's, whose is probably the kindest of glimpses.

The culprit.

He must be.

No chance it's anyone else.

Before long, class commences and I'm forced to endure the length of the period without any clue as to how this situation escalated so quickly.

I shouldn't be so surprised; however, I'd like to understand the chain of events that brought us to this moment, this reality.

The answer is obvious. I call it HSD. High School Disease.

Can you guess what the symptoms are?

Anxiety. Depression. Fever accompanied by chills.

And those are on the milder side of the spectrum.

I can feel myself starting to hyperventilate.

Heart palpitations are not my favorite.

I knew this would happen.

So what's next?

What's there to do?

Breathing would be helpful here. Elongated, chest-expanding exhales. One at a time.

Too bad I feel like an elephant sat on my sternum. The tightening constriction of my airway continues.

Odd thing is, as much as I detest Ryan for putting me in this oh-so-envious situation, I also want to jump his bones and plant one on him.

Crazy, right? Hormones and heart strings are a recipe for emotional upheaval.

Just as I'm starting to get my bearings and focus my gaze on Ms. Lopez, a student TA walks into the classroom with what appears to be long-stemmed red roses. From what I recall, these are purchased by the student body as part of a fundraising initiative for the dance. You buy a flower and have the option to include a personalized message with it.

So cheeseballs, but cute in theory.

The kid delivering them awkwardly ambles to the front of the class to interrupt our lesson.

He has about half a dozen to pass out.

The second name he reads out loud is, you guessed it, mine.

My initial reaction is to let out a brief guttural laugh.

So subtle.

Then I look down at the table in front of me and hope because I'm avoiding eye contact, no one can see me either.

Wishful thinking.

Trey, the messenger, saunters over to my desk and casually lays the red, red rose and accompanying hand-written note in front of me.

I feel my cheeks turn a shade that matches the rose in front of me.

Not wanting to make any sort of uncouth gestures, I wait until Trey passes out the rest of the lovely gifts before peaking at the card, which is folded neatly into quarters and perfectly creased at the folds.

Deep breath.

I open the card slowly, as if opening a literal Pandora's Box.

First thing I notice is the handwriting. I'd describe it as Courier New meets Monoscript. It reads:

Heyu—

Just had to send you one of these because they are pretty cool and smell good…just like you. Can't wait until Saturday =)

Xoxo Ryan

Knots instantly form in the pit of my stomach. My mind oscillates between thoughts of *aw that's cute* and *eww that's creepy.* Did he really just comment on my pheromones?

I remember that the author is sitting across the room and can probably see my facial expressions.

Which likely betray my thoughts. Or so I'm told.

I glimpse up in his direction to confirm my suspicion.

Yep, he's studying me like a Picasso painting.

I manage a faint half-smile before averting my eyes towards the teacher.

Throughout the lesson—something about character development, honestly I can't remember—Alex and Charlie blow up my cell phone with inquisitive combinations of bitmojis.

My favorite is the one with the brain exploding.

Gossip is the fuel of feminine feels.

When the bell rings they charge over to me like toddlers during a game of freeze tag.

"So?!" they chant in unison.

"So…?" I love messing with them.

"SAM!" Everyone within earshot turns to look.

"Subtle, ladies," I grab my purse and books, and of course, my rose.

They chase me out of the classroom and down the hallway towards my Bio class.

Meanwhile, I spy Ryan keeping a safe distance behind us, safe being the operative word.

Smart kid, that one.

"We want deets! What does the note say?"

"What a romantic gesture. I didn't think boys had the hutzpah to court women in that way."

"It was very nice," I reply shortly.

"Girl, what's wrong with you? He's a *senior*. You've struck gold."

That's an interesting way of looking at it.

"Don't you have practice to get to?" I'm on the verge of annoyed.

"Buzzkill," pants Charlie. "Text us later?"

"Always do."

As they scamper off back down the hallway and towards the gym, Ryan, hands inserted into his front pockets, moseys in my direction with a half-scared, half-eager look.

Damn he fine.

"I see you got my message," he nods to the flower clutched in my left hand.

"Oh, this is from you? I couldn't read the handwriting."

"Well, let me decipher it for you," he smiles that knee-weakening smile. "I'm really looking forward to hanging out with you this weekend."

"Don't take this the wrong way, Ryan, but may I ask why?"

His smile fades to a look of confusion.

"Haven't we already had this conversation?"

"Not that I can recall."

"Smooth, Sam."

I wink.

"Why is it so hard for you to accept I want to take you out?"

Wow, this conversation took a turn for the serious.

"I wouldn't say *that* ..."

"What would you say?"

I need a minute.

"I'd say there are a lot of layers that may require a more thorough explanation than I could cover in what's remaining of this five-minute transition period. These layers include topics related to societal norms, cultural intelligence, and teenage daughter-y, to name a few. Perhaps it's something we can discuss … on our date … on Saturday …"

Ryan looks at me, somewhat stunned. Truthfully, he shouldn't be so surprised. At least now he has a better idea of who he's dealing with.

"I look forward to it. Have a good class," he bids as he grabs my free right hand and brushes his lips across my knuckles.

Oof, that's hot.

I wonder where he's taking me. That would be a good thing to find out.

Wardrobe implications.

"Where are we going?" I call out somewhat sheepishly.

"It's a surprise."

This is obviously his first rodeo with an underclassman. Amateur hour.

"Don't take this the wrong way, Ry, but surprises don't fly well with the mothers of 14-year-olds who are hanging out with almost-legal senior boys. Just saying."

He strokes his chin, as if in mock consideration of this notion.

"Point taken. Let's meet at Main Street by Balboa Pier, near the Ruby's sign by the parking lot. Say six?"

"See you there."

Probably. I reserve the right to abort this mission at my discretion.

CHAPTER EIGHT
IT'S THOSE LAYERS

'm actually going through with it. This *date.*

Mom was really cool about it. I'd basically kept her up to speed on my interactions with this sleuthy senior and so she wasn't surprised we reached the point of male-female ritual.

I'm a little surprised, but that's another story.

"He sounds like a nice boy. Are you excited?"

"Excited? Sure. More nervous though. He's … like … old. I'm not sure I'll be able to keep up."

"Sam, the last thing you should be concerned with is your ability to keep up. It's the boys that should be worried about keeping up with *you.*"

For a host of reasons, we decide NOT to loop Daddy in on this inaugural event. We're basically doing him a favor.

I haven't had much exposure to the buffer sex. The progeny of

69

an Indian father and an all-kinds-of-white mother, my experience with cultural constructs is nothing short of *mixed* messaging. Pun intended.

"No dating," says my father in his 30-years-an-American-citizen Punjabi accent. "You're too young. You're too fragile. You can't handle it.

"School is really important. You can beat everyone at school, especially the boys. That's how you will be successful."

So, I can dominate the academic competition but not go to dinner with a boy? Talk about conflict. My mom often plays the mediator, waving the white flag for truce on the omnipresent topics of Friday night activities, make-up, and midriffs, among other things. More often than not, it's best to not have the discussion. Sometimes that becomes a bigger issue.

My dad takes an opposing position as compared to many fathers in his home country. In India, many girls my age are discussing arranged marriage and the future of the family wealth, not academic achievement. Relationships between girls and boys are not readily discussed in my family, at least between my dad and me. I've seen Bollywood movies; I know how it works. *Bride and Prejudice* didn't receive national acclaim for no reason. The song "No Life Without Wife" represents the cultural practice well—and with qualified humor. Daddy wants his girls to be educated. He's already established funds for all three of us kids to go to school debt-free. I admittedly lack the intellectual fortitude to understand what this means, but I am nonetheless grateful. As far as I'm concerned, our—my and my sister's—participation in an arranged marriage was never an option. I'm sure my parents had a more serious discussion amongst themselves, one of many conversations I'm not privy to.

In addition to his protective instincts, Daddy also has a temper. Charlie and Alex have seen his ire in action. One time, we got in a fight about what time I had plans to go meet my friends for a movie—*Hustlers*, I think—on a Friday night. I must've yelled, or something, because he got up from his chair (not typical) and boomed at me, "Well I guess you're not going to the movie, then!"

Message sent.

Naturally I stormed off hysterically crying and didn't talk to him the rest of the night. But we made up in the morning. We always do. We share short tempers and even shorter paths to forgiveness.

Sometimes I don't understand what he expects. I've hit puberty. I've also been a good, no, top, student, as in 4.6 GPA top. And yet the amount of protection he insists on qualifies as borderline suffocating. I doubt Bro will go through this. He's only nine. He's probably watched less than I am.

And—let's be real—saving us the headache of explaining that dating does not a long-term commitment or act of deflowering make.

These secrets are exhausting. That's what they are—secrets. Do I wish I could tell my father this kind of stuff? 100%. But not at the expense of living my best life.

That's one of the complexities of growing up in a multicultural household. Not to mention living in a predominantly white, upper-middle-class neighborhood.

I'm pretty sure my siblings and I make up at least half of the Indian-American population at that school.

School, school, and school. Those are our priorities, in that order.

Notice friends, relationships, and fun do not make the top three.

I have my friends, my (pseudo) relationships, my fun. In the way that I know how and can manage against.

Not gonna lie, it's isolating when my peers partake in certain rites of passage—school dances, dates, parties—that I need to rationalize and beg for.

And so, I choose my battles.

Ryan, at this point, is not one of them.

I feel guilty, making Mama choose between being open with her husband or her children. It sounds dramatic, and, well, it kind of is.

I'm sure there are things I tell Mama that I'd prefer she not share with my dad. But that's the curse of childhood. I'll outgrow it eventually.

For now, I prefer to live in denial.

And worry about my upcoming date.

I've never been on a date before.

It's kind of intimidating.

"Eat a salad, it's clean eating and you won't get cheese all over your face," Alex offers.

"Wear something cute but not like you're trying too hard," coaches Charlie.

Thanks ladies, super helpful.

Last but not least:

"Just be yourself," Mama says.

Which version? I think to myself.

Perhaps that's just the problem—I'm overthinking it.

Ryan may be right. Why is it so hard to say yes?

It's those layers.

CHAPTER NINE

CHALLENGE ACCEPTED

"Have fun, hunny. Try to enjoy yourself."

My mom knows me so well.

My heart is imploding on the inside. My right eyelid is twitching slightly.

Normal side effects of a high-stress situation for Samantha Selim.

I crack my neck one last time, take a deep breath, and grab my purse.

I chose a flattering red top, fitted at the waist, and a pair of dark denim jeans as my ensemble. Not to mention my Rocket Dog wedges. Only by being five-foot-three can I get away with such obnoxious footwear.

I lean over to open the car door, and lo and behold, Ryan is standing not ten yards away, eyeing my every move. He stands comfortably, knees relaxed and unlocked, arms casually tucked into his front pockets—his default stance, I'm learning.

As we lock eyes, he offers a kind smile, somewhat goofy yet honest. Funny thing is, neither of us look away.

Intriguing.

"You look beautiful," are the first words out of his mouth.

"Don't start with me," are the first words out of mine.

Did I really say that?

Good thing he laughs, in a way that seems to be natural and not forced. Thankfully.

I sheepishly walk over to him, my gait somewhat hampered by the anxiety weighing on my chest and somehow manifesting in my feet.

Maybe it's the shoes.

Ryan, unencumbered by any sort of nerves, grabs my hand and brings it to his lips. He leaves an innocent peck, nothing more, nothing less.

So he's somewhat consistent.

"I'm glad we finally get to do this," he offers. "I'm looking forward to getting to know you better."

"Likewise," I reply. "So, what's up first?"

"First, I thought we'd grab dinner at none other than Ruby's. After that, I figured we could walk around, maybe go to the arcade, get some ice cream—"

"You've given this some thought," I interrupt.

"I like to have a plan."

You and me both, I muse to myself.

"Hungry?" he asks as he offers his arm and another ridiculously cute grin.

"Starving." I take his arm and follow his lead towards the restaurant on the pier, where we will share our first meal together.

Oh, firsts. This is a night of firsts—my first date, my first time lying to my dad.

Okay, so that latter isn't *entirely* true, but as it relates to a boy, it's the truth.

It's too early to tell, but being around Ryan is surprisingly soothing. Not surprising in the *I didn't think it was possible* way, but in the sense that I feel at ease and, dare I say it, myself.

It's early, but it's obvious I have all the feels.

"So, tell me about your family."

Oy—sensitive territory, and we haven't even gotten to the apps yet.

"Well," I stall as I collect my thoughts. "I'm the oldest of three. I have a sister and a brother. Sis and I are sixteen months apart, Bro is five years younger than me. My parents came to Orange County via unique paths. My mom is originally from North Dakota, the oldest of six. Her family moved to LA because her mom got a teaching job back in the 60s. My dad came to the US from India, by way of university. He moved to Anaheim after living in Boston for 10 years. He got over the cold."

I pause to gauge Ryan's interest in my narrative so far.

He's not glassy-eyed, so I guess that's a good thing?

I march on.

"They met at a brokerage firm in Irvine in the early 80s. My mom was the broker, my dad, the client. Match made in trading heaven. Been together ever since. Are you bored yet?"

Personally, I never get tired of this story. My parents are amazing.

They both grew up on farms surrounded by open land full of wheat fields, living the small-town life.

They are both the oldest of their siblings and share the value of responsibility.

They are both self-made and worked hard to make their livings.

They both value education and supporting their children.

They are my heroes.

"On the contrary," he says, sounding like a Brit in a non-pretentious kind of way. "I find your story very compelling. Not like most Newport girls. You're the prodigy of immigrants, and I don't mean that in a derogatory way. It's unusual, and I mean that in the best way possible. Don't shoot me," he says as my face furrows into a WTF facial.

"I think I understand what you mean. I had quite the identity crisis growing up. Still do, if I'm being honest."

That's a black hole waiting for its next victim.

"Oh yeah? Do tell."

Walked right into that one.

"Well … Honestly it's kinda tough growing up in a household ruled by two different sets of cultural standards. My mom, for example, understands the dating thing, boys and girls, hormones, yadda yadda. My dad, on the other hand, doesn't think we should be alone with a boy until we're 30. 'We' being my sister and I. So, you can see where there can be a conflict, especially given that we grew up American, and what comes along with being American. Does that make sense?"

"Absolutely. I can see where it would be tough to navigate. It's not that there's right and wrong, it's just … different. How do you reconcile the two?"

"Exactly!"

Wow, he gets it.

I continue, "I feel either way, I'm not meeting some kind of expectation for what a good daughter should be. That's a lot of pressure. Perhaps there's a layer of it that's self-imposed, but truthfully, this is the reality I'm living in. It's like I don't own the decision or choice to participate. Sure, I'm just a teenager and under the jurisdiction of my parents for another four years, give or take, but I feel like it's deeper than that. It's a question of identity, of introspection, of self."

"Damn, you're deep."

I knew it, I went too far.

"It's refreshing."

What?

"Not many people analyze their thoughts the way you do. I feel like I've learned a lot from you already, and we haven't even gotten our milkshakes yet."

This place is infamous for its Oreo-cookie malts. My favorite.

"High praise," I *cheers* with my cherry cola.

"I mean it. I haven't met anyone like you."

"What, half-brown half-wonderbread?"

Obviously that's not what he meant, but I feel like being facetious.

"That, and someone with the courage to explore who they are, and wander into foreign territory that is just that, foreign. That's a scary thing most people aren't brave enough to take on. I admire that in you."

I'm so cheesing right now. I keep going.

"It's the duality of hope and fear. Most times we make choices out of fear, out of a pursuit for self-preservation, avoiding the risk of the unknown. I try to choose hope when I can. That's where we grow … also acknowledging growing pains are a thing for a reason.

"I think Nelson Mandela said it best: 'May your choices reflect your hopes, not your fears.'"

"Samantha Selim. Who are you and where did you come from?"

"I'm going to assume that's a rhetorical question." That's my default response to any question I have no intention of answering.

"How about, I'm so grateful to spend this time with you. I'm really enjoying myself."

"It seems you have good taste."

And with that, our chili cheese fries arrive. I hesitate, remembering the oh-so-sound advice of my gal pals.

Meh, live a little, I tell myself.

They're SO good.

"Now it's your turn," I say, turning the tables in the subtlest possible fashion.

"There's not a whole lot to tell," Ryan leads. "I don't say that to avoid answering the question—I know that's what you're thinking."

"Good guess."

"I say that because I'm the literal definition of typical, of a type representative of Newport Beach-ity."

"How reductionist of you." Clearly, I'm not having it. I have a totally different conception of this specimen, and I'll be damned if it's all but the antithesis of my impression. I can't possibly be that off-base.

Could I?

"Good catch, Selim, glad you're paying attention."

I feel something that resembles rage yet also amusement permeate through my body. I pause, waiting for him to continue his clever biography.

His smug demeanor irritates me.

"Don't get me wrong, sometimes I feel like that, for lack of a better term, basic Newport bro. I surf, I do CrossFit, I eat tacos on Tuesdays. It's a fairly predictable lifestyle.

"I do, though, find it hard to relate to people. It's like I'm just not interested in most of the things I'm supposed to be interested in. Like booze, pot—I like sex, though."

Noted.

"Sometimes I think it's a maturity thing, but I know I have my moments. I don't find the same things interesting or funny or worth my time."

"You're an old soul."

This is not hard to figure out.

"Wow, you figured that out pretty quickly."

"And you didn't?"

"I don't really see it that way … until 5 seconds ago."

"How do you see it?"

"Like I'm an oddball with no default friend group."

"That seems … kinda harsh." I'm not quite sure what to think as I speculate.

"I don't mind it, I just don't think it's a typical experience to be having these thoughts and feelings about my social experience in high school. That's all."

"This whole conversation is atypical, in general," I offer.

I'm only half-kidding.

"Cheers to that."

This time we toast with our malts, savoring the goodness of our Saturday night therapy session.

By the time the rest of our food arrives, we transition our chat to lighter topics, like what we like to do for fun, how we spend our weekends, and the like.

I learn Ryan has a flare for the written word. Or so he claims.

"I enjoy writing, I consider it to be a kind of release."

"What do you write?" I inquire.

"This and that," he offers sheepishly.

"Nice try. What have you written?"

"It's kind of all over the place. Some short stories. A screenplay. Poetry. Depends on my mood."

"I'd love to read your work some time. I like to write too. In fact, I write movie reviews for the *Newport News*. I started doing them when I was eleven. I keep a journal too. My mom likes to remind me that John Steinbeck based his works off of his personal journals. He's one of my favorite authors."

"You are full of surprises."

"You ain't seen nothing yet."

After dinner, we make our way towards the Fun Zone, where the arcade lives alongside the ferris wheel and ferry boats—the nominal "fun" the namesake suggests. We stumble upon one of those old school photo booths next to the ice cream shop—and by old school I mean one that isn't digital.

Obviously we have to try it.

Ryan, on the other hand, takes on a sheepish persona. Quite unlike the person I've engaged with to date.

Intriguing.

"What? Are you afraid the camera is going to steal your soul?"

"Hey, that's a thing! Some Native American cultures believe that to be true."

I know this. I'm testing him.

"Is that so?" I offer wryly.

"Why do I get the feeling you knew that?" He smirks.

"Because I did."

I peel back the curtain to the booth and nestle myself in front of the lens. Ryan follows closely, and attempts to relocate me away from what would be the center of the photograph.

Attention whore.

"You're in my spot!" I pout.

"What are you gonna do about it?"

"Challenge accepted."

With that, I begin tickling his side body, anticipating this would be a weakness.

I was right.

He buckles like floorboards during an 8.0 earthquake. It's almost too easy, until he counters my effort with a headlock and bearhug at the same time.

I walked into that one.

"Okay, okay," I pant, "you can have the spotlight."

"Thank you," he says smugly yet graciously. "It's all yours. I just wanted to touch you."

Honesty. How refreshing.

"Imagine that," I muse. "We both get what we want."

We proceed to take what amounts to three strips of photos, each strip including four unique images.

We make silly faces, sad faces, pose in Bonnie and Clyde fashion. They turn out quite cute.

A memento for the occasion.

Before we know it, it's 9:50 p.m.—ten minutes to curfew.

Ryan notices first, and politely suggests we make our way over to the predetermined meeting spot where Mama dropped me off some hours ago.

I appreciate his commitment to "the plan;" I take it as an indication of his values, right or wrong as that might be.

Reminds me of my dad.

That's a scary thought.

Scary in the sense that I always expected I'd end up with someone—and at least date a majority of men who—is the antithesis of my father in most ways.

I'm only 14. There's a very big chance that I am wrong.

Not because of my youth, but statistically speaking I have way more years of life ahead (if I'm so fortunate) to inform these thoughts.

I digress.

We wander over to the base of the pier, plop down on one of the city benches, and wait. Ryan migrates his hand to the top of my knee.

He looks at me tentatively, seeking permission.

He takes my silence for tacit compliance.

"I had a great time tonight," he whispers, dare I say somewhat predictably. "I'd really like to continue to get to know you."

"What's to know?" I respond, with a wry smile so he knows there's an element of humor intended.

"Everything," he says, quite seriously, in fact. His gaze lingers as his face moves closer to mine.

"Oh," I manage to stifle. I can feel his breath on my cheek. It's minty fresh.

Holy crap, he's going to kiss me.

Out of instinct, I turn my face away from his, but he won't have it.

He reaches over to turn my cheek towards his, gently, yet with purpose.

"I'd really like to kiss you now," he states.

"I gathered that," I say, somewhat pedantically.

"Okay. I'm going to kiss you now," he tries, again.

"Okay," I concede.

As his lips brush against mine, I feel a distinct shiver throughout my upper body. His arm is around my shoulder; his grip tightens as he draws me closer to him—not in a possessive way, but in a manner synonymous with protection, safety.

I like this feeling.

The kiss itself lasts for about five seconds. As our lips part, we look at each other again, wondering how the other is feeling in that moment.

I gather it's one of shared satisfaction.

No more than three seconds later, I catch a glimpse of my mom's car pulling up to the curb in front of the bench where we're sitting.

Oh God, is it possible she saw us?

I jump up and flee Ryan's embrace without a moment's hesitation, and start bolting towards the passenger side of the car. My hand is on the door handle when I come to my senses, turn around, and say my goodbyes.

"Thank you for a lovely evening," I say loud enough so my mom can hear.

"The pleasure is all mine," Ryan sweetly surrenders as I take a seat in the car, and he closes the door behind me.

"Did you two have a good time?" Mama asks us.

Through the open window, Ryan answers, "The best."

"Good night, Mrs. Selim. Night, Samantha."

As we drive away, I nestle back into my seat and look over my left shoulder towards Mama.

"So?" she questions. "Is he a good kisser?"

I decide that's a rhetorical question and change the subject.

CHAPTER TEN
GUARDED

My mind is racing when I get home. As I prepare for sleep, I cannot stop thinking about the night's earlier events.

What was *that?* Is the predominant theme of my thoughts.

Ryan's company was pleasant, the conversation, thoughtful and kind. Why am I so conflicted?

Our life is what our thoughts make it, according to Roman general Marcus Aurelius. Why do my thoughts revert to questions rather than answers?

I'm struggling with how to feel. He seems so pure of heart and full of spirit. And yet, I'm haunted by my vulnerability and the secrets (?) I shared.

Why am I so guarded?

Likely the product of my nature and nurture—who I am, coupled with how I grew up, and the variety of influences in between.

As I lay in bed in an attempt to enter a slumber and escape

the day, I shelter my anxiety in a dream of romantic bliss, which roughly translates into lots of making out and slightly inappropriate hand placements. Boobs, crotches, you get the gist.

What will Monday bring? A question as much as a musing. Alex and Charlie will no doubt accost the poor soul. I've already been inundated with texts from these two temptresses—from the second I un-"Do Not Disturb"-ed my phone.

> *Did he buy you dinner? Did he get*
> *handsy with you? Does he smell*
> *good? What did he wear? How*
> *often was he on his phone? Pics?!*

IT NEVER ENDS.

I just want to chuck my phone in the ocean and avoid this unnecessary wake of wonder.

And yet, I'm also somewhat obsessing over the possibilities.

Oy, the teenage dream.

Monday returns for its weekly visit. As far as I'm concerned, this is the longest Monday of my life.

I will say, I've never been greeted with such pomp and circumstance as I was on this day.

As we pull into the pool parking lot, Alex and Charlie perch on the hood of Alex's car like chickadees waiting for Mama Bird to come home with breakfast.

I wonder what they're waiting for.

"Samantha Selim, you can't ignore us forever!" Charlie chants in her sing-songy tone as I power walk past the car and towards the gated entrance.

How I wish that weren't the case.

"Did you two have a nice weekend?" I respond, intentionally avoiding the ginormous elephant in the pool parking lot.

Alex and Charlie exchange glances as they follow me in vehement pursuit, before looking in unison at me with a standard "for real" smirk.

"We had a very nice time," I offer, naively hoping these six words keep these vexy vultures at bay.

"You liiiiiiiiike him," Alex postulates. "I can see it all over your China doll face! Girl, you can't hide that love."

"Love? We went on one date! Plus, I'm technically not allowed to date." I keep walking towards my locker. The first period bell is (hopefully) about to ring.

"Semantics," Charlie inserts. "The real question is if you want to see him again."

"Honestly," I begin, "I'm not sure I do."

"Porqui?" Alex maneuvers her body in front of me and stop me cold in my tracks.

"Because you're stressing me out!"

"Oooooooh," they muse. "Message sent."

Charlie gives me a wink as she whispers her parting words, "I hope he's a good kisser."

I love my friends.

I'm on edge most of the day. Not that I'm avoiding Ryan.

Okay, I'm avoiding Ryan.

I didn't hear from him on Sunday, which, I never know what that means—hearing from or not hearing from a date following a date. I could Dr. Phil the crap out of that situation and never make a definitive determination.

So I'll avoid the prognosis all together.

I make it to fifth period without any un/expected encounter. Approaching drama class, I take a few deep breaths and exercise some yogi asana before entering the classroom.

Ryan is nowhere to be found.

Good? Bad? Happy? Sad?

A sigh of exhaustive, cumulative disappointment, I feel.

Oh, well.

After class, I make my way towards Bio. Before I turn the corner, I sense a hovering figure attached to my shadow.

Abruptly I turn around, and there he is.

"Hi," Ryan salutes, charmingly accompanied by his wholesome smile. Those pearly whites are rather distracting.

"Hey," I manage. I have nothing more substantive to offer.

"How was the rest of your weekend?"

Enveloped by inner turmoil, I ponder.

"Good, how about you?" I rethink my reply.

"Lonely," he shares. "I really enjoyed hanging out with you on Saturday night. It made Sunday seem dull by comparison."

The cheesiest of cheeseball. Do people really say that?

"Lonely, huh? Meaning you immersed yourself in some serious surf and hung out with your bros all day?" I sound insulting.

Ryan lets out a chuckle.

"That, AND I wrote you something."

Oh, dear.

"You wrote me something?" I repeat, making a poor attempt at hiding my not-so-subtle shock.

"Yeah, I wrote you something. Check your email."

I pull my iPhone from my back pocket and open my Gmail. Sure enough, an unopened message from HeSurfs949@gmail. com sits atop my inbox.

It's titled *Our Night*.

Uh oh, I'm in trouble.

My heart palpitates as I click on the email and read:

The night was perfect, under the stars.

Your tender eyes and bright smile healed by scars

That represented my pain and weakened my heart,

And through your words you whispered we would
    never be apart.

Your lips touched mine, in that mystical kiss.

And all that entered my mind is eternal bliss.

I knew from that moment you would always be mine,

And our love could only strengthen through time.

The sunset was beautiful, just like your face.

And the walk was enchanting, in your warm embrace.

The night is one I will always remember,

One that will rest in my soul forever.

Dude, that's DEEP.

What a way with words this idealistic boy has.

I'm stunned. Speechless. My mouth hangs agape in disbelief. I'm emotionally oscillating on the spectrum of "OMG, how sweet" and "Danger, Danger."

"Oh," I stifle, searching for the appropriate exclamation. "I had no idea you had … so … many feelings."

I'm such a jerk.

"Neither did I," he concedes. His glacier-blue eyes flicker from mine to his black Vans slip-ons. That was unnecessarily kind. I don't deserve it.

"I was wondering if you'd want to go to a movie with me this weekend? That new Marvel movie comes out and I've been wanting to see it since the first previews."

Yikes, this guy doesn't give up.

"Maybe," I muster. "Can I let you know?" I can't come up with a good excuse on the spot.

"Sure, you can let me know," he's not the least bit fazed. "Have a good sixth period, I'll talk to you later."

"Okay. Thanks for the poem."

I'm trying (and failing) to be polite.

He winks, effortlessly as he does, retraces his steps, and disappears around the corner down the hallway, away from me and my ineptitude.

A few moments pass before I collect my bearings and re-engage with reality.

What. Just. Happened.

Can I really be that insensitive? I am THE queen of empathy, or so I used to be. Have I been dethroned?

I consider if I'm being hard on myself. After all, how could I have anticipated this gesture? I haven't heard from him in 45 hours.

Could he be a traditionalist? Someone who appreciates the digital divide and respects the notion of personal space?

I haven't met one of those in a while. Truthfully, I'm the only one I know of at BBHS.

The greater issue is, do I reciprocate these feelings? Or, even less resolutely, do I wish to explore what could potentially be *feelings*?

Now I have a headache, one of the throbbing variety. My pulsating temples beat melodically in tempo akin to "Bohemian Rhapsody."

And now I have to sit through an hour-long lecture on cell sex and reproduction. How appropriate.

When I get home, I regale Mama with the afternoon's events, and show her the literary masterpiece Ryan has crafted in salute to his teenage hormones.

"Hunny, this is so sweet," she exclaims, wholly moved by his work.

"Then you date him," I quip, clearly spiteful of Mama's complimentary support.

"Sam, now, dear, no need to be so dramatic," she consoles in the way only she can. "This boy wrote you a poem. He didn't ask you to marry him."

Thanks for pointing that out, Mama.

"Are you going to respond back?"

"Respond …?" I consider what this entails.

"Yes," she states matter-of-factly. "Are you going to write one back?"

Dear God, she's lost her mind.

"Why would I do that?" I wonder aloud, also hoping she will fill in the gap I so obtusely cannot close myself.

"Because you like him, too."

That's what I was afraid of.

"I do?"

"Yes, you do."

Oy.

"Because he sees you."

I know exactly what she means. We have that kind of relationship.

He sees me. Not just my half-Indian, half-Wonderbread bag of bones, but also—at the risk of sounding sorcerous—my soul.

I can't get over how at dinner he empathized with my point of view, my perspective, my story.

How someone could have such purview into my thoughts and experiences? Especially mine? I'm an odd duck.

It's unnerving.

He scares me. I don't like being scared.

"Why don't you give him a chance?" Mama suggests, in the soft way only she knows.

"What does that mean?" I beckon. "Go out with him?"

"Well, no, because you can't *date*," she winks as she

emphasizes that last word. "But get to know him better. Like I said, it's not like he asked you to marry him."

"But this is *high school*, Mom. I've been harassed plenty as it is."

"At the end of the day, Sam, it's up to you. I just don't want you to have any regrets."

BOOM. She nailed it. Like only she does.

Blast, that woman. I hope I become half the woman she is.

Why do I care so much about what people think? It's the teenage nightmare. I much prefer the teenage dream.

Where's Katy Perry when you need her?

When I share the poem with Alex and Charlie, I get a *slightly* different reaction.

Fearing a papertrail perpetrator, I elect to read the poem over FaceTime.

I sound way more anxious than I actually am (I think).

"Girl, he wants your body," Charlie, as only she does, puts into the universe. "Poetry is like song lyrics. Boys only write to get laid. It's a simple fact."

Okay, Charlie. Sound logic.

"Obvi he's into you," leads Alex. "I think the question is whether you want to accept it and what that means."

Oddly profound, Alex. I'm a little rattled at the intellectual depth of her response, to be honest. I don't mean that to be any kind of commentary on her intelligence.

Maybe it is. But it's not intentional, like that makes it any better.

Awareness and acceptance are two different things, though interconnected in many ways.

Awareness, as I see it, is the ability to look inside yourself and identify the things that make you who you are, objectively and without judgement or bias.

Acceptance, then, is the *courage* to accept what you find out about yourself, and the understanding to embrace the implications for how to live your life.

There are parallels to the duality of hope and fear that I ascribe to, almost like a religion.

When us kids were born, my parents decided not to raise us with any sort of religious affiliation. They wanted us to choose for ourselves, of all things. While I appreciate the sentiment, by the time we got old enough to understand the role of religion, our values and moral code were pretty much already formed.

Mom was raised Lutheran; Daddy, Muslim. They share a moral code they clearly imparted on us that transcends Jesus and Mohammed.

(Can we just appreciate how two people from opposite sides of the world found each other, fell in love, and built the life they did? It blows my mind.)

Mom has framed artwork of the Serenity prayer, which she never drilled into us but had casually displayed in our bonus room. It reads:

God, grant me the serenity to *accept* the things cannot change, *courage* to change the things I can, and wisdom to know the difference.

In hindsight, it's kinda funny how this poem captures so succinctly what I believe, though I grew up without the context of theological teachings surrounding it.

Getting back to Alex's point—she's right. I'm aware he's into me. That's not the issue. The issue is my acceptance of his feelings, the situation and all it entails, and what that means for me.

Let's say I accept them, his feelings. What do I do with those feelings? How do I move forward?

So I ask my girls, "How do I accept my feelings?"

The FaceTime medium doesn't really allow for the thoughtful responses like text, Gchat, or email might.

Charlie blurts, "It's not that hard. You just … accept them. Ya know?"

So profound.

Alex's two cents are a bit more … helpful.

"Well, hun, I personally think you need to make a choice. Do you want to pursue this guy or not? Think about it like one of those decision trees on Pinterest. Take the emotion out of it. Knowing you, that's what's tripping you up."

She's not wrong.

I'm the most emotional person I know.

"How do I take the emotion out of it when that's literally how I make my decisions?"

An innocent question, and certainly one that needs answering. Maybe not today; consider it a life-long conundrum.

"Life begins at the edge of your comfort zone," Alex recites.

"You sound like one of those wall art quotes," I comment.

"Doesn't make me wrong," she reasons.

Touché.

"Basically, I'm being a pansy and need to make a decision to not be a pansy. Si?"

"I think that sums it up," chimes Charlie, mostly for dramatic effect, I gather.

"If you don't want to be a pansy, then yes," Alex takes her stance.

"Fair," I sigh. "Loaded with lots of logic to think about tonight. I think it's time for me to say goodnight. Chat you later."

I tap out of our FaceTime call and collapse on my bed, facedown. I inhale deeply, and admittedly, choke a little on my own breath.

Turning over onto my back, I make a second attempt at filling my lungs with freshly circulated, A/C-infused O2, mixed with salty sea air you can't avoid in our house.

I did better that time.

Laying there, submerged in my pillows and stuffed panda bear collection, I revisit the day's conversations with my female confidants. Peace is a casualty of my thoughts. The interworkings of my brain light up like headlights on the 405 during rush hour on a Friday evening.

My mind has always operated like this, like an unmapped constellation of a universe unexplored.

And yet, I feel a sense of calm.

Perhaps it's the breathing exercises.

Perhaps it's my commitment to my peace, my truth. Knowing what I need and pushing myself to get it.

Guess we'll find out.

I think I need some sleep.

CHAPTER ELEVEN
PERSONAL PSYCHOLOGY

The next day, I reset.

I reset my mindset, my anchor of reference to the high school experience.

Granted, it's not as simple as flipping a switch. I've simply made the choice.

Now comes the hard part: adjusting the behavior to reflect this choice.

After fifth period, instead of sheepishly retreating from the theatre, I walk up to Ryan as he packs his backpack, which resembles a turtle shell when he wears it. I have my L.L. Bean tote and Alta coffee cup in tow.

"Hi."

I'm so bold.

"Hey, Sam," he greets. His voice is so melodious. "How's it goin'?"

"Not bad," I offer. "I'm looking forward to going home and

taking a swim. The water's been so warm lately. Did you surf today?"

"Actually, I did," he continues, somewhat chirpy in his reply. "You're right, the water has been warm. The waves sucked though, a little choppy for my longboard."

"Perhaps tomorrow will be better," I chime, ever the optimist.

"You're such an optimist."

Thank you, Captain Obvious.

"Speaking of optimism, I would like to take you up on your offer for a movie this weekend. Would Saturday night work for you?"

Another date night. I'm living on the edge with that one.

"Oh, really?" he asks, explicably surprised by my proposal.

"Is that a rhetorical question?" I pander. Here we go again.

He pauses, cocks his head to his right, and studies me. Boy, does he study me.

"Saturday night, it is," he confirms.

"Sounds good," I smile.

"Does it now? How about that …"

Date (?) No. 2 comes and goes. Not in a bad way, by any means.

We end up going to a movie, not my favorite choice for an outing, simply because the conversation tends to be limited by nature of the environment. Unless you're a miscreant who prefers disruption to dream sequences.

We are not those things, at least on this night.

Following the movie (another superhero special—I won't ruin the show for you), we walk over to the bookstore somewhat adjacent to the mall. Bookstores are not-so-secretly some of my favorite places to get lost, not only physically but mentally.

My favorite section, depending on the bookstore, tends to be the aptly titled "self-help" section. Personally, it feels a little misleading. I would describe it more as "personal psychology" rather than the negatively connotated "help" word choice.

Let's be real: everyone needs *help*. Some people are simply more attuned to their needs than others. Cue awareness and acceptance. I sense a theme.

Ryan seems to have most of himself figured out. That's high praise for a seventeen-year-old. It's early, sure, but when it comes to high schoolers, self-awareness is fairly obvious to assess. Maybe it's just me.

For the record, his favorite section is history. Also old soul-ish.

I rest my case.

Time is so fleeting. And yet, some moments linger like overcast clouds on a summer morning. Again, not in a bad way. It just is what it is.

I, none too surprisingly, enjoy our tit-for-tat conversation and subtle jabs. Verbal sparring at its finest.

I kinda like him.

Now that that's been established, we move along on the flow chart that is teenage romance—teenage romance for girls with strict fathers.

My dad, for as long as I can remember, abhorred the idea of me and Jenny dating. Or hanging out with the rougher sex, for that matter. Encounters were not supported, encouraged, or, dare I say, tolerated.

When I was in third grade, a couple of my male peers decided it would be fun to pull my hair. I was wearing two braids that day, and each boy stood on either side of me and yanked. Not so hard that it caused me physical pain; the gesture itself deserved retaliation.

I told my dad about this encounter when I got home from school that day.

The next day, Daddy appeared on the blacktop during recess. Let's just say his visit wasn't related to getting in on a game of handball or Foursquare. These days, it was acceptable for parents to simply show up and visit their kids during break. At Balport Elementary, it was especially easy, since the school bordered the beach on one side. (How fortunate we were to attend one of two schools in the WORLD that shared a boundary with the coastline.) Gone are those days of wayfaring. Now all visitors must check-in at the front office and receive a badge denoting their visitor status.

Daddy walked down the sidewalk and onto the blacktop where my friends and I were playing handball. Once I noticed his shape hovering by the basketball courts, all five of us went to greet him.

I ran up to him as I did, and embraced him around the mid-thigh area, as far as I could wrap my arms given my vertical challenges at age ten.

He returned the gesture, as only dads can.

"Hi Sammy," he greets. "Where are these boys giving you trouble?"

Oh. I see.

I look around the playground and spot the culprits, Eric and Carter, playing kickball on the far side of the yard.

"Over there, Daddy," I point out the two third graders wearing their Quiksilver t-shirts and skater shoes.

"Can you tell them I'd like to talk to them?"

Oh. I see.

My gal pals and I run over to the kickball court, all too proud to say that my dad would like a word.

Or rather, my dad wants to kick your ass.

As the boys sheepishly approach my father's looming figure, I can't help but feel bad for them.

Then I get over it.

My dad, not one to sugarcoat, gets straight to the point.

"If you ever touch my daughter again, I'm going to throw you in the ocean. Do you understand?"

Bet they never heard that before. Those poor boys.

They never screwed with me again.

My ten-year-old self found that to be entertaining. Still do, in fact. Daddy was my Superman. He still is.

Sometimes, though, I find the cultural divide to be more of a thrashing ocean than a steady river. More often than I probably recognize or care to admit.

In the Indian culture, dating was not a concept, at least when my dad was growing up. Marriages were pre-ordained and arranged between families—a symbol of alliance and respect.

My mom says that given the absence of this social stage, the default position became "no, they can't date"—they, being my sister and me.

Which, I can understand, in theory. It's the execution that becomes elusive, especially when hormones and Homecomings are thrown into the mix.

I can certainly comprehend parental concern and all that entails, but there's also a thing called life I'd like to live. I also recognize this is one chapter in the novel that is my existence. Even so, there's those hormones. Biology is a force to be reckoned with.

It doesn't feel like there will be a tomorrow. It's a pipedream, a fantasyland. I can only imagine what tomorrow will look like. I doubt it will look anything like Disney's rendition. Too many spaceships and robots. Although, I guess we are living amongst drones these days. Everything is possible.

I'd describe our household as patriarchal. The fe/male boundaries are starkly contrasting. It's not good or bad. It's just, what *is*.

What also is, is the pervading perception by a father of his daughter's interactions with a (slightly older) Newport Beach lifeguard, approaching college age.

My internal debate, between bosom and brain, centers around what extent I share him, share Ryan and the joy he brings me, with the man who had, to date, been the only man in my life.

It's a new boundary to bridge, an indication of my coming-of-age, no doubt. I think that's what they call it?

I err on the side of downloading Daddy, but I'm also afraid he won't understand. It's important to me he understands. But can I control that?

Me and my rhetorical questions.

Power and control are two of those ephemeral and eternal states, a contradiction in terms. Sometimes I feel life is a contradiction in terms. And I'm only 14.

Ultimately, in the grand scheme of life, what's the harm in introducing these two men among men? Their acquaintance could, on a spectrum, range from quick and dirty to trite and tangled.

Oy, the possibilities.

I guess we'll see.

CHAPTER TWELVE
MISSION ACCOMPLISHED

Against my better judgement, I invite Ryan over to our house to hang out and "go for a walk." Which essentially means make out, walk a few steps, and make out some more. It's a literal trail of kisses. The French would be so proud, oui?

"Are you sure you want me to meet your dad?" Ryan asked, assuringly yet with slight hesitation in his baritone voice as we walked out of Alta.

"I am, are you?" He says my snippety chides are my best quality.

He gives me a look, one dressed in irony and capped with affection, blended with a spicy vanilla chai latte. What a doll.

"Yes, I am. I just want to make sure it's the right time."

"Is there ever a right time to meet the father of the girl you're seeing—"

I catch myself, as we haven't yet had *the talk*. Whoops. So much for being suave.

"It's nice to know we're seeing each other, at least," whispering as he wraps his right arm around my shoulders.

I tremble a bit.

"At least," I chide as I turn my face towards his and steal a quick peck. "It was touch and go for a while, but in the end, you turned out to be okay."

Wink, wink. Nudge, nudge.

Did I mention he also appreciates my sarcasm? Part of my charm.

We strategically decide Ryan will *casually* stop by the house after a morning surf session on Saturday, the day after tomorrow. Since he typically surfs at Blackie's—a local spot about a mile from our place—we figure it's a less intrusive, more opportune meet-cute, given the synchronicity. After all, synchronicity is a wink from the universe—even if conspired by two love-struck teenagers.

How's that for self-awareness?

"Speaking of which, Babe," I lead in, "I wrote you something."

That's right, *I* wrote *him* something.

From the back pocket of my denim cut-offs, I retrieve a thrice-folded sheet of paper, type-written with a poem I wrote, especially for him.

It reads, in 11-pt Montserrat:

The One
By Samantha Selim

Do you see it?
I realize that now I do.

A man of a beautiful spirit
is how I'll always think of you.
Your sapphire eyes are so engaging;
they melt my heart away.
And from that voice that relieves my pain,
I know you're here to stay.
The smile that shines across your face
lights up my world like the blazing sun.
And from the way your hands find mine,
I know that you're the one—
The one that gives me comfort
and the one who will never go far,
For you're the one I want to be with
to look up at the stars.
<3

In assured order, Ryan's mouth, at first agape with an emotion somewhere between shock and sham, subtly puckers into a soft pout that finds my own.

Savory and satisfying.

"I wanted to write a rebuttal to yours," I squeak, uncharacteristically sheepish in my delivery.

"Mission accomplished," Ryan concludes. "Hunny, it's beautiful. Thank you, truly, thank you."

I sense a hint of pride in his voice.

Aww.

"We should show your dad!" Ryan teases. "He should know what a great writer you are."

"Don't worry, he already does."

When I was in first grade, my dad went to my parent-teacher conference, where the teachers give the parents the inside-scoop about their kid's performance, whether they'll survive the year, etc.

My first grade teacher, Ms. Miller, shared a piece of my writing with Daddy during their all of 15 minutes together.

"I've never seen any student write like this, at this age," Ms. Miller disclosed.

I wasn't there, but I like to think that made him smile a little.

Will he smile when Ryan makes his acquaintance?

My money is on *hell, no*.

Honestly, I'm not quite sure what to expect. It's terrifying, actually. The planner in me suffers a pinching paralysis in times like these.

We shall see soon enough.

CHAPTER THIRTEEN
HE'S THE BOSS, SO...

Saturday arrives innocently enough.

Mom takes me to yoga class, per our weekend routine. She gets her coffee on while I get my meditation on. It works for us.

On the way home, we pick up donuts from the local coffee shop. Daddy likes his sweet treats. Whenever we get Indian food from the market cafe in Tustin (our favorite), he brings back the best desserts. My favorite is *kaju ji barfi,* made with cashew nuts and milk, topped with silver varq. (It's *real* silver!) *Gulab jamun* is also tasty, made with khoya, fried golden and dipped in saffron-induced sugar syrup—the Indian version of donuts. We're greasing palms, as the saying goes.

We find Daddy sitting as he does—left leg propped perpendicular to his right—in his favorite spot on his favorite sofa. He rests his right hand on his right quad, and holds his chin with his left. Looking out onto the sand, lost in thought, this man is always thinking.

By this time, it's almost 11 a.m. Ryan's usually wrapping up his session around this time.

He has his routine, too: after exiting the water and returning to his white Tacoma pick-up truck, he pulls his car keys from the secret spot in his tailpipe. He towel-changes from his wetsuit into a pair of boardshorts and a t-shirt, along with his Rainbow sandals. This whole process takes him about 20 minutes, inclusive of chit-chat with passersby regarding the day's sets and weather forecast.

At 11 a.m. on the dot, I receive a text that says,

The seagull has left the shoreline.

Corny and cute. Just my style.

As assured and smooth as I possibly can be, I *casually* mention my friend Ryan is in the area and plans to stop by on his walk.

And by casually, I mean panicked and pansy-ish.

Daddy doesn't seem to notice, though. The only response I get is a subtle, "Hmmm."

I'll take it.

I'm so focused on my own heart palpitations I don't give it much thought.

And so, what seems like an eternity passes, and Ryan appears perched on the front steps of our patio, bleached-blonde hair slicked back with sea water and these hideous sunglasses that make him look like a Backstreet Boy clone—in their prime years.

Still, I find my heart aflutter.

Apparently, my type is surfer boy.

He kind of hovers near the entry gate for a long few seconds before purposely approaching the front slider that opens up into the living room, right where Papa Selim sits.

I sing-songingly chant, "Daddy, look, Ryan is here."

Greeting Ryan at the slider, I glide open the glass door and offer a "Hey, how's it going?" in the most unhurried cadence I could manage.

"Mr. Selim, it's a pleasure to meet you, Sir," Ryan doesn't waste any time with the introductions.

Anxious beyond reason, I glance towards my dad, eager to see exactly what his reaction might be to this salacious salutation.

Mind you, it's only salacious in my mind—because only I know what ulterior motives are baking behind those charming eyes.

Oy, are they charming.

What feels like eons go by. During this time, I absentmindedly guide Ryan to the opposite sofa to sit down and offer him a beverage (I think?). Honestly, I forget. It's like when you're driving somewhere and all of the sudden you arrive, but you can't remember how you got there.

At least this is (physically) safer.

We sit down and wait for Daddy's acknowledgement of our presence. I temper my internal energy by breathing, as I learned in yoga.

It helps, but only mildly.

In reality, it's probably about seven seconds that go by before the impending silence is broken.

"Ryan," Daddy softly addresses the boy to my right, "how are you?"

What do we do with that?

Open-ended introductions have so much opportunity to lead a first impression amiss. Part of me wonders if this is intentional.

I'm so cynical.

"Well, Sir," Ryan begins, "it's a beautiful day in Newport

Beach. I can't say I'm feeling anything but blessed. I got a good surf in this morning, and now I'm here talking to you and your beautiful daughter. I really can't complain."

Seriously? He had to add in *beautiful daughter.* While that *may* be (subjectively) true, I'm thinking it's not the most necessary content to include in an initial dad/dateable boy meeting.

But that's just me.

Daddy, thankfully, smiles a little, almost encouragingly.

"How are you doing in school?"

I physically hold myself back from letting out a guttural laugh.

Ryan looks at me with a blank stare, as if he's caught off guard.

Didn't I warn him?

"Oh, yeah, school …" he manages. "I really like English, I'm not sure if Samantha has told you but I like to write. I'm not a big fan of math and science, but I get by."

"Samantha said you're a senior? Where are you going to school next year?"

Uh oh, the killer question. I should've prepared him for this.

College is a big deal in our household. The culmination of our studies is a first-class ticket to a top tier four-year school, be it UCs or Ivys, per our father's roadmap to success.

Junior college is not an option.

"I'm planning on going to OCC for a couple of years, then transferring to film school, probably USC or UCLA. My dad went to USC."

Good move, sliding in that last piece of info.

"You don't want to go now?"

Oy, saw that one coming.

Ryan looks at me, a little unnerved by the personal nature of these questions. What can I say, Daddy is not a student in the art of subtlety.

"No, not now. I'm not ready, Sir," Ryan softens.

"Do you have the grades?"

"Honestly, I was never very good at school. Like I mentioned, I've always liked English, and that's where I tend to do well. I don't have the GPA right now for the schools I want to go to."

"Hmm, I see."

Silence.

"I'm sure you'll get to where you want to go," Daddy offers.

I feel the need to dig Ryan's grave right then and there.

Ryan isn't fazed. "Thank you, Sir, that means a lot."

Taking matters into my own hands, I intercede with some fluff about what a pretty day it is, that it's about time for us to leave on our walk.

"Go enjoy the day," Daddy beckons, "there's no better place to be outside than here."

"It was great to meet you, Sir, I hope to see you again soon," Ryan gets up to shake Daddy's hand. Daddy doesn't get up—too comfortable, perhaps—but offers his hand to Ryan.

"Bye, Daddy, we'll be back soon."

We don't say *I love you*. That saying is reserved for Mama. It's a Papa Selim thing.

Speaking of Mama, we catch her in the kitchen on our way to the back side of the house. She's sipping her coffee—2% plus one Splenda packet—while reading the paper in her favorite spot at her bistro table. She loves it, she says, because in this location, she can see both her plants and the ocean. Best of both worlds.

It would be inane to assume she didn't hear any of the dialogue that just happened in the living room.

"Hello, Mrs. Selim," chimes Ryan. He nods his head in respect as he greets her. I don't know why, but he has this certain fondness for my mom. His mom is from Oklahoma—perhaps it's a Midwest thing?

"Hello, Ryan," Mama reciprocates. "You met Ashar today, didn't you? How did it go?"

She knows how it went. She can be manipulative like that, not in a malicious way, but in a power play kind of way. She does it to me sometimes and I don't even know it's happening. Sis has to point it out to me. It's one of my blind spots.

"It was good," as generic as an answer can be, toots Ryan. "Guess we'll see if I passed."

"I'm sure you did fine," Mama consoles. "What route are you taking on your walk today?"

A graceful change of subject, Mother.

"I was thinking the bayside today, Ry doesn't spend a lot of time over there, aside from his LG days at 18 and Bay."

He gives me a look. The *and Bay* towers are typically covered by the rookie, non-tenured lifeguards; they are located, as the term implies, *on the bay.* Not exactly Wedge status.

"What?" I play dumb. "It's the truth."

"Ah, yes, the truth," Ryan repeats. "What a multi-dimensional concept that is," smirking as he helps himself to a buttermilk donut.

I must say, I do dig his comfort level. No shame.

Mama just laughs as she says, "It's easy to see why you two get along so well."

Ryan and I look at each other, tacitly complying with her observation.

Very astute, this woman. Glad I have her genes.

"We'll be back in a few hours, Mama. Love you," I grab an old-fashioned glazed donut and scoot towards my mom to give her a hug and kiss before departing.

Notice the distinction in goodbyes between Mama and Daddy.

One of the many nuances of a biracial household.

"Take your time, we're having chicken curry for dinner," Mama confides.

Unlike those in our local community, we eat a lot of curries, always infused with turmeric and cumin spices. Turmeric possess an inherent staining quality; I'm not a messy eater, but for whatever reason, you'll know I've had chicken curry to eat by looking at my top; yellow blotchy stains take the form of various shapes you can making a guessing game out of, like an alternative edition to the cloud game. Daddy taught Mama how to prepare these specialties, and now she's better at it than he is.

The base of practically everything we cook is olive oil and onions, sprinkled with chopped garlic—all things that encourage heart health. Mama lets this mix simmer on the stovetop for ten minutes or so in a large pot, like you would use for soup or stew. Then she adds chicken, usually thighs (more flavor) with the skin removed, and her vegetables of choice. We typically add tomatoes, cilantro, and peas—these go in last, about ten minutes before the dish is done; otherwise they get mushy. She also adds the seasonings—coriander, cumin, Lawry's salt, turmeric—and water, so it doesn't burn. The amount of water depends on how much curry you want to have, the ratio of solids to liquids. The whole process takes about forty minutes or so, with variance depending on portion size, stove heat, etc.

We usually eat our curries over rice. My dad always teases my sister Jenny because she *loves* rice. Naan or tortillas are also good for dipping if you're into finger foods. Mama also makes *raita*, which is a yogurt-based condiment made with cucumber, cumin, and mint. I personally mix it all together—the curry, rice, and *raita*—into my own smorgasbord. Daddy calls it the Sloppy Samantha. Honestly, it tastes the best the next day, after the flavors have had time to seep and marinate the vegetables and meat. Leftovers are a best-kept secret when it comes to Indian cuisine. Sometimes I'll take some to school for lunch and nuke it in the cafeteria; more often than not, the smell causes some confused looks. I, the culprit, usually remain anonymous. Less aromatically, I am partial to the exotic fruits Daddy brings home for us to eat. My favorites are papaya and mango, which I could eat every day for the rest of my life and not be mad about it.

Ryan and I make our way out the back entrance through Mama's garden and out to the alleyway. We hang a right and walk towards 11th Street, where the crosswalk cuts Balboa Blvd. I feel my gait's pace quicken; subconsciously, I'm aborting a mission gone wrong. Ryan doesn't seem to notice. He probably thinks that whole exchange went well.

Oh, the naïveté of teenage boy.

As we approach the crosswalk, he proves my hypothesis.

"I think they like me!" he announces, boldly and without hesitation.

"Of course they like you, babe," I affirm, "that was never the question." I peck his cheek, my lips garnished in donut glaze.

Ryan pauses, clearly suspicious of my response.

"What was the question, then?" he retorts, unnerved by the direction this conversation is about to take.

"The question is about whether you're good enough for their

daughter," I state with confidence yet tempered with a gentleness only my loved ones would ever see.

"Isn't that the same thing?"

Perplexity isn't very becoming. Neither is ignorance.

"Well ..." I contemplate my words as wisely as my 14-year-old self might allow. "They're not mutually exclusive. You can have one without the other."

His spirit visibly changes from soaring to stunted.

"Let's hear it, Sam," Ryan stokes. "What's the bottom line here?"

I can't stand being put on the spot. I detest the inherent improv of it all. We know I'm a planner; this doesn't work for me.

"It's hard to know for sure, but knowing my dad, he probably wasn't super thrilled about your college plans. And I say that with the premise that all he's talked about since we could read was how important college is—"

"It's not like I'm not planning on going," he interrupts my monologue. "Didn't you hear that part?" his voice booms in that baritone pitch I usually swoon for, but at this moment I'm borderline resentful of his reaction.

"Please don't yell at me," I politely counter.

"Sorry, Samantha," he grabs my right hand and brings it to his lips for a conciliatory kiss.

"I know you're planning on going," I continue, "your plan just isn't the same as his plan. And he's the boss, so ..."

I purposefully trail off, to allow him the courtesy of filling in the blank himself. But also, so I don't have to state what should be so obvious.

"What does that mean for us?" His earnestness melts my

heart.

"As far as I'm concerned, it doesn't affect who we are, together," I proclaim. "It's our life. I'm not worried if you're not worried."

I smile as tenderly as I can, hoping to convey my support of our relationship. A few months ago, I wouldn't have pictured us here, in this place—both physically and literally. And yet, here we are. (I need to reread my journal entries. That should be a hoot.)

Life is funny like that.

I'm still getting to know Ryan, I accept that. But these feelings I have aren't solely driven by hormones. They couldn't possibly be.

Could they?

As I filter my thoughts, Ryan stops in his tracks.

"What's wrong?" I beckon.

"You're just so beautiful," he solemnly discloses. "How did I get so lucky?"

Whyyyyyy is he so cheesy?

Gotta admit, I kinda like it.

"Your cheeseballing might have something to do with it. Full disclosure."

With that, he slides his right arm around my waist and locks in his hold on me, like a hook and eye fastener. He pulls me close, so that we're hips on hips. His left hand cradles the back of my neck as he gently encourages a meeting of our lips.

"I am so glad I met you," he whispers.

I quiver.

"You have no idea."

CHAPTER FOURTEEN
"FUN"

It's not in my nature to sneak around and cryptically answer my parents' inquiries. Obviously it's their right as the keepers of my existence, at least for the next 4-ish years, to ask me whatever they want. I like to think we have solid, open communication. I have no reason to hide.

And then, one night, that changes. I've never understood how that happens. But it does. It's like watching SportsCenter for 15 years straight, and then one day losing interest and not turning it on. A scary phenomenon. Something to ponder.

I digress.

I'm home on Tuesday night before winter break starts. Which means, roughly translated, teachers are muscling in as many tests as possible so we don't "forget" the content over the two-week hiatus.

Their reasoning, not mine.

While at home, as per my usual Tuesday routine, I'm studying in my room for Mr. Mason's geometry test. Subject matter includes something about triangles. I feel like the whole semester has been about triangles; they should consider renaming the class *Triangles and other things*.

I've always been good at math. Daddy made sure of that. Coupled with my near-photographic memory, I dominate at multiplication tables. I won Around the World *twice* in third grade. Obviously I'm still proud of that. I've also had a lot of practice, definitely more than the 10,000 hours touted by the theory of the same name that's been tossed around over the last few years.

As I'm reviewing the mathematical mysteries of Pythagorem's theorem, I get a text that reads:

> *come outside*

Um, yes, Master?

I don't respond well to commands. Ryan should know better.

And so, my reply contains:

> *what will i find? That will dictate*
> *my next move...*

Call me a feminist, but I'm not interested in the alpha-male, machismo mindset/action/behavior combo. It's just not for me. Though I've never considered if that alternative might be a little boring. An internal dialogue for another time.

Ryan replies, true to form:

> *the man and musings of yur dreams*

It still shocks me how well he knows, or at least anticipates, my triggers.

In my navy Loft sweats and white tank top, I slither through the hallway, down the stairs, and do my best to peek out towards the boardwalk. The sun sets around 5:30 p.m. this time of year, and by now—just after nine—the sky is a velveteen blanket strewn with balls of fire. Our patio lights make viewing anything beyond our property line difficult to see.

My dad has long since retired. He usually goes upstairs before 7 p.m. to watch David Muir and *Jeopardy!*, which of course I watch with him. Mom is a bit more of a night owl, and truthfully the one I'm most watchful of at this point. It seems she's in the midst of her TCM binge for the evening. Her personal abode is the space at the back of the house, once our playroom, so to speak. The female version of a man cave.

While she's immersed in the latest John Wayne rerun, I float towards the front slider and steal a peek behind the gossamer curtain. There, not ten feet from our front patio, stands Ryan, holding what I can only imagine to be an Oreo-cookie shake from Ruby's.

How thoughtful is he?

Also, how brave, considering my dad is asleep directly above where I'm standing.

I, as quietly as I can, step outside the door and close it behind me. I'm mindful of my gait, as I don't want to appear *too* eager—for him or the milkshake. Perceptions can be deadly.

"Is that for me?" I ask, innocently.

"Depends," he taunts.

"On?"

"On how much you like this poem."

From the side pocket of his boardshorts, he pulls out yet another folded sheet of paper.

At this point, I think I'm desensitized to the romanticism infused in his gestures.

I read to myself:

Waves bring joy to those who desire
A chance to surf a set of fire.
Surfing is a dance in which the wave leads
The surfer along his dance floor, the sea.

The sparkling, blue mass of water presents
A horizon in which hues pain dramatic sunsets.
The surfers look at this view as a guide
To their dreams that follow through to a heavenly ride.

"It's so...melodious," my pathetic attempt at praise. Truthfully, it's one of his better works. And of course, it's about surfing. I haven't seen much aside from his short stories and screenplays. And of course, his poems about me.

Writing is one of those things that connects us. We share a proclivity for the written word, an appreciation for diction. I'm a sucker for a man with an extensive vocabulary. It's one of Ryan's better traits.

"You like?"

"I like."

"The milkshake is yours," he concedes. "Clearly I would give it to you anyway, but I like the word *melodious*, so it made it that much easier."

See, he likes big words too.

"Also …" he continues, "I have this."

He shows me his keychain, with, shockingly, a set of keys on it.

"Is one of those supposed to be the key to my heart?"

I'm so funny.

"Well, one of them is the key to the tower …"

Tower, meaning the lifeguard tower. In front of my house. 100 yards away.

Oh dear, I know where this is going.

"So, you want to go to the tower?" I lead in. "Into the tower, and …"

"Have some fun."

I freeze. My body drops to the temperature of the Oreo-cookie shake I'm holding.

At this point in my life, I've never gone past first base with a guy. In fact, Ryan was first base. Now, apparently, he's looking to steal second; hell, who knows—even third or home.

I'm not terribly comfortable with this. My instinct is to run inside my sanctuary and abort the conversation, and potentially the relationship, all together. Might seem a little unfair. This is the first time any sort of sexual innuendo has finagled its way into our conversation.

I shouldn't be surprised, though. He's seventeen and tickled with testosterone. Exhibit A: his hormone-infused poetry.

I have my own biological battles to fight. This is where our age difference just might be an issue. I wonder if he's still a virgin. I highly doubt it.

This is a whole other level of unknowns I wasn't even thinking of when I made the choice to pursue this love affair. I feel dumb.

All these thoughts are layering themselves in a lattice formation inside my brain, while Ryan stands stiffly in front of me holding his keys.

"Fun …" I'm terrible at buying time for my thoughts. "How are we defining fun in this context?"

I sound like an academic deciphering the existential meaning of a good time. Sometimes I am too much, even for me.

"I was thinking we could experiment and explore a little, you know, get to know each other on another level."

So that's what they're calling it these days.

"Do you want to have sex with me?" I'm not usually so candid but in this situation, desperate times …

"Is that a trick question?" His face softens with a delicate smile only he can manage. "Of course I do. Look at you! Do I think we should today? Not necessarily. We've never talked about it, so now I guess is as good a time as any."

"Meaning, when you offer up a lifeguard tower to experiment and explore? That kind of time?"

"So maybe my approach wasn't so graceful, fine," he admits candidly. "But how does one actually broach the topic of sex with someone they actually like-slash-love?"

Damn it, he said *love*.

"I've never done it before, so please forgive me for my poor delivery, Sam."

This is a lot for one evening. AND it's past my bedtime. When it rains, it pours, and hails, and nor'easters. I wouldn't be surprised if the ground shook a little, too.

EARTHQUAAAAAAAAAKE!!!

I feel myself sliding in and out of consciousness. I'm confuddled by his choices of words. Never done what before? Had sex? Said I love you? Both? It's a tad unclear.

"Can we sit down?" I finally muster. "I have questions and I would like to articulate them somewhat intelligently. Let's go over here," I strongly suggest as I take his free hand and lead him to the city sidewalk bench under the shining lamppost half a block away.

Hurriedly, I collect my thoughts and sequence my questions in a way that makes the most sense, sense being the operative word.

We sit, and the first words out of my mouth are:

"Why do you love me?"

Nice job, Samantha. Way to kill the moment.

"Way to cut to the chase there, babe," Ryan chides, in the least accusatory way possible. "Shall I count the ways?"

Cheeseball central over here.

"It comes down to the fact that I can be myself around you, absent of fear and judgement. You make me feel safe. Do I think you're hot? Of course. Do you make me laugh? Absolutely. But foundationally, I love you because I can be me when I'm with you. I'm what I think is my best self around you. And I love you for that."

Pause.

"Does that suffice?"

I really want to cry, but to date, crying has never gotten me what I wanted. To be clear, these would be happy tears. But as a result of *The Selim Family: The Early Years*, the act of crying carries a blemished connotation.

And so instead I smile, so quintessentially a Samantha move, wistful yet strong.

"It more than suffices," I whisper as I scoot towards Ryan and prop my legs over his lap. "I was just making sure you could reasonably articulate it."

I wink in an overly animated way. "You passed."

"I'm happy to hear that," he says gently as he leans in for a quick peck. "So, safe to assume, no tower tonight?"

I exhale, in my mind. Thank you for that.

"I think that's a good call. Another time?"

I have no intention of considering an alternative opportunity to pursue this … aspect … of a relationship. Not tonight, at least. I'm just not ready.

But Ryan doesn't need to know that. Not yet.

For now, I enjoy the Oreo-cookie goodness of my milkshakes and cuddle closely with my kindred spirit who loves me on a sidewalk bench on the beach.

How romantic.

CHAPTER FIFTEEN
SEASON'S GREETINGS TO ME

The holidays are a blur. Two weeks of school-less days means plenty of time to shop, sleep, and sneak off with Ryan.

I don't *really* sneak off. It's more like a few (or seven) late night rendezvous on the tenth street corner under the lustrous lamppost. It seems to be a bit of a routine.

One evening we spend navigating the serpentine sidewalks that hug the bayside, catching glimpses of the city's annual boat parade between stolen kisses.

My favorite boat float is the Bad Santa that goes shirtless with a pair of oversized red suspenders and shouts PG-13 epithets at onlookers. I'm surprised he keeps getting invited back. Not exactly an idyllic illustration of holiday cheer.

Christmas in Newport is one of my favorite times of the year. While we lack the opportunity for an emblematic White Christmas, we offset that with festive lighting and a limited number of tourists. It seems every house has some display of colored confection strung from each pillar and plank. I have a soft spot for the icicle lights that twinkle as if they're melting down the edge of the house.

Strolling along one of these nights, Ryan stops abruptly and hooks my left arm, as delicately as one possibly can.

"I just want you to know, I love you," he declares, somewhat dramatically.

"I know, hun," I acknowledge. "I love you, too."

His blonde hair contrasts starkly with the night sky, which mimics tones of obsidian.

"Good, just want to make sure."

He pauses, somewhat uncomfortably.

I'm starting to feel somewhat uneasy.

"Are you worried about something?" I ask. "You're acting really weird."

Don't sugarcoat it, sweetheart.

"I'm fine," he musters. "I think I'm just conflicted about the conversation we had a few weeks back."

What conversation? I take a beat to consider the variety of topics we've explored in recent weeks—we *are* talkers, he and I, so it's not exactly an exigent diagnosis.

Oh God.

I'm such an idiot.

Without overacting, I (seemingly) ask in a calm manner, "What conversation is that?"

"The sexual one," he offers explicitly. "To be honest, it's been on my mind a lot."

"What parts, hun?" My innocence can sometimes get the better of me.

"Well, for one, I can't stop thinking of having sex with you."

I guess I can't blame him for that.

"That's very flattering, Ry, really, I'm flushed. But you know I'm not ready. It's … just … not the right time. I'm too young."

I'm too young? Who am I?

"I understand that, really I do. I just wanted to tell you what's going on with me, that's all. Don't worry, it's not a big deal."

Don't worry? He's dreaming.

We resume our walk towards the boats where the neighbor's dingy hosts a DJ playing "Merry Christmas, Happy Holidays."

The rest of the night I'm lost in a torrid storm of doubt and debilitation.

Seasons' greetings to me.

Typically, I spent New Year's Eve in the company of my girlfriends. Either we'll go to one of our houses and hang out while watching all the TV specials, or stay in with our families.

This year, Ryan and I pass the evening by watching *Endless Summer*, a 1966 documentary about—what else— surfing. It basically follows two surfers around the world, hitting all the major surfing destinations, known and undiscovered. Ry, the ever-avid surfer, goes to another place every time he watches this film.

Or so he reports.

This is my first time seeing it. While I'm all for watching men clad in skin-tight neoprene, there's something about the pace of an instrumental soundtrack that is *kind of* boring.

I wouldn't share this feedback with Ryan. He'd probably just ignore me anyway.

There's something sacred about surfing that only those who participate in it connect with or understand. I guess you could say it has cultish culture qualities. But doesn't every following en masse?

Like me and my yoga crew.

I think overall there are lifelong benefits to identifying with and participating in community activity, regardless of theme or content. It's a distinctly human need, ingrained since the invention of fire and, thus, a focal point for gathering and living.

I digress.

At the end of every year, I make a list—a list of things I'm happy about from the preceding year, what I'm not so happy about, and what I'm looking forward to in the new year. They're somewhat resolution-ish, but an expanded version, if you will.

This year, mine looks like this:

- Happy for ... meeting Ryan, starting high school, continuing my yoga practice, my loving parents, my journaling practice, time with people I love, time to myself
- Not so happy about ... not being able to date (openly and honestly), peer pressure
- Looking forward to ... building a happy relationship, getting good grades, loving my family, learning to do a headstand

Sometimes I surprise myself at how much of an old soul I actually am. Other times, I'm totally aware and embrace it.

This New Year's has a different feeling, almost a shift in

subconsciousness.

I bet you a million dollars Ryan has something to do with it. To be honest, I'm disappointed in myself for having these feelings. I'd like to think I'm good at drawing boundaries and prioritizing my own goals and aspirations sans the crippling effect of young love.

Ah, young love. I'm in trouble.

Not the parental discipline kind of trouble. Historically, my parents and I have a good thing going, a mutual respect, higher in their favor of course. There's an understanding there.

Truthfully, it's an interesting commentary on the biracial dynamics of our household. I hardly *ever* get in trouble. I'm a rule-follower, as we've established by my incessant need to abide by the terms dictated by governing forces—whether that be friends, family, or faculty.

That's not what is distinctly dapper about the whole thing. My dad is what we can call the Enforcer, the keeper of the chaos, the patron of patriarchy. My mom is, alternatively, the Ally—the companion, the agent, the all-things-associate. Where Daddy would discipline, Mom would adjudicate.

I guess you could say they have the good cop/bad cop thing going, but there's another dimension to it. It's more about their commitment to each other and to us, the kids, the apples of their collective eyes.

As products of seemingly contrarian upbringings—my dad in Middle Asia and my mom in the Midwest—these two make the best team. And I'm not just saying that. There's something to the agrarian attitudes people from small towns share, the partnership and commitment to morals and values.

Mama and Daddy each grew up in the light of religious narrative, Mama a Christian, Daddy a Muslim. Their families, from what I can tell, demonstrated their own version of commitment to these narratives, resulting in their own codes of morals and values.

I recognize that these foundations are not unique to my family unit; what is unique is how they found each other and built this life for us by writing their own narrative. I will be eternally proud of that and vow to continue that legacy of that narrative.

I digress.

Today, I'm in the kind of trouble that is present at the frontal lobe of my brain, the center of information processing, but for some reason my actions are not informed by and disregard this information.

Exhibit A: I decide it's better to spend NYE with Ryan over Alex and Charlie, who got tickets to see (some EDM artist) at the Rose Bowl. I prefer to not immerse myself in a computer-generated ruckus while people around me are tripped out on E in a euphorically altered state. Once again, a testament to the nature of my old soul.

And so we watch our full-length feature of a surf film and retire around 10 p.m.—a whole two hours before the ball metaphorically and literally drops. He's an early to bed, early to rise type, too, though there are some days where exceptions are not only encouraged but necessary.

So far, it's the only flaw I've identified in Ryan.

I sleep well this night, refreshed by my newly acquired jasmine-scented candle and sherpa blanket I got from my mom for Christmas. New Year's Day falls on a Sunday this year (as does Christmas, per the calendar quirk) and so on Tuesday, we go back to school.

Oh joy.

I spend New Year's Day on the couch watching the Rose Parade on repeat followed by college football, per tradition's terms.

While lounging on the couch, also per tradition, I receive a bunch of texts, mostly gifs and bitmojis, wishing me a happy new year.

I return each message with a heartful reply. Meaning, the token "Thanks! :)" What's missing, though, is a conspicuously absent note from Alex and Charlie.

Strange …

My heart quickens, just a little, as I settle back into Miami and Alabama's blood bath. College football can be an analogy for my life: pressure and palpitations.

Happy new year to me.

CHAPTER SIXTEEN
ICE ICE BABY

As I suspected.

Ice ice baby.

With the onset of Tuesday came concurrently an arctic chill that permeated the pathways in and around campus. At least, that's how it felt to me. It felt like everyone was wearing sherpa vests and Ugg boots to manage the cold. Granted, it's January; it's also Southern California. Sixty-five and somewhat sunny. We are predictably irrational. Dan Ariely would appreciate that.

Mama drops us off and we follow our typical route through the regal gates and part ways—Sis to her locker, and me to mine. I don't see Alex or Charlie in the parking lot, where they usually stake their claim.

Approaching my locker from the south side of the row, I see the girls chirping away, as if eons had passed since their last gab fest.

I swivel around the boy's water polo team, dodge the drama kids, and glacially approach my friends. I'm sensing *something is not right*, as Madeline's boarding school teacher Miss Clavell would say.

"Good morning, you two. How have you been?"

Immediately I notice my choice of words indicate a noticeable amount of time has passed since our last real conversation, clearly a faux pas according to girl code.

It's like I'm openly admitting I ditched my friends for some dude. Without admitting anything.

Even before I can process these thoughts, Alex and Charlie take one look at me, turn on their heels, and walk away, leaving me standing there.

It's like I have the plague or something. I've never seen two people abort like that. Like the Millennium Falcon at warp speed.

Needless to say, I'm in total shock. Panic might be a better word. A wave of fear washes over me, like a tsunami over a grom totally unprepared for what s/he's experiencing. At least I'm not being choked by salty seawater. Silver lining?

I stand there for a moment, shaking like a leaf. But also paralyzed with fear.

I'm thinking about who just witnessed this act of abandonment and what *they* might be thinking.

What did she do? Must've been pretty bad.

Damn, these high school chicks are unforgiving.

She probably has bad B.O. I would walk away, too.

My gut reaction: retreat to the girls' bathroom and regroup.

I wish I could say I hold it together.

But that would be a lie.

As soon as I close the door to the farthest stall from the entrance, I sit on the toilet seat and weep like there's no tomorrow.

I choose a bathroom location at the corner of campus very few people frequent, so I don't need to worry about anyone hearing me and getting a teacher.

Even in times of crisis, my mind retains its strategy-oriented default. It helps somewhat.

I consider texting Ryan, but I don't think he'd understand. He's a dude, simple as that.

He'd also probably find the girls and rip them a new one. I don't need that right now, especially if I want to salvage the friendship.

Why would I salvage the friendship?

They were so mean, like Regina George mean.

Honestly, I didn't think high school girls could be that cruel. I could never be that mean to anyone, other than my sister. But that's a whole different thing. We're blood and have a mutual understanding of unconditional love. We have established boundaries. I thought Alex, Charlie and I did, too.

Maybe they're jealous? I mean, they're cute, they get a lot of unsolicited male attention. It's not like I'm impacting their access to the retinue of dudes that is our high school demographic. 65/35 easy.

Even if they are jealous, how could they let something like this interfere with and potentially compromise our friendship?

After a few more dry heaves, I collect myself and my belongings. My eyes are a little bloodshot. I wash my face with lukewarm water, grabbing the edges of the water bowl from time to time to steady myself.

The bell rings. I can hear the scampering to first period begin. I won't see the girls until after lunch during drama class.

How appropriate.

And Ryan will be there.

Cue the fireworks.

Speaking of Ryan, I decide it's time to text him and fill him in on the morning's events. Curious to hear what his response will be.

> *hey, I had an interesting encounter*
> *this morning with the girls. meet*
> *you at break and fill you in?*
>
> *Good morning, beautiful.. What*
> *happened?*
>
> *I'd rather tell you in person, if*
> *that's cool*
>
> *Okay, have a good class. See u at*
> *the pool after 2nd* 🤍 🤍

Then ensues the longest two hours of my life. I have Math and English, each class requiring usage of a different side of the brain. My brain, in particular, is warped with feelings of rejection, isolation, fear, anger, loneliness. Throw in some hormones and it can get ugly.

I get through the classes unscathed; I manage to avoid having to speak at all. It's my lucky day. Thank you, Universe.

Ironically, this is the same Universe that allowed my recent ostracism to take place. There's that duality theme again.

I find Ryan at the entrance to the pool, amongst his cohort of California fellows. His stance is one of measured savoir faire with a slight hint of shyness. Hands in pockets, and that silly turtle-shaped backpack (which I secretly love) perched on his deltoids, he hovers on the perimeter of his clique, until he sees and darts towards me.

"Hey gorgeous," he says as takes my right hand and greets me with a quick peck. "Deets me."

I stifle a laugh before I launch into my monologue de misery. Between panting and pauses, I try to assess Ryan's reaction. He calmly waits until I'm finished, a cool 30 seconds or so later.

"Honey, it sounds like they're just being bitches," he rationally states. "They're probably just mad you're not giving them as much attention as they're used to getting from you. And quite honestly, they're probably a little jealous."

Jealous. There's that word.

"Why do they have to be jealous?" I pine. "Why can't they just be happy for me? I'm always supportive of them." I sound like a whiny teenager. If the shoe fits, I guess?

"Because," Ryan begins. "They're not as enlightened as you are, babe. Or as mature. A flower does not think of competing with the flowers next to it. It just blooms."

"You got that from *Mulan*, huh."

We love our Disney movies.

"Ancient Chinese proverb," he clarifies. "And yes, but that doesn't make it any less true."

He has a point.

"So you're saying, they're annoyed with my bloom?"

This is my subtle attempt at bringing humor to an otherwise hurtful situation.

"Yes, babe, your bloom is too bloomy for their egos."

That made me feel better. Not healed, but better. I recognize that I can't control how and what people think and feel, even if I do have the best of intentions. It's like our judicial system: if someone commits a crime and causes harm to someone else, even if it wasn't full of malice, intent doesn't matter.

How pertinent.

"It's like you always say, Samantha: focus on what you can control. Now's the time to practice what you preach."

Ryan throws me a wink before using two hands to wrap around my shoulders and pull me into a long-overdue embrace. I think physical touch is one of my love languages.

"Want to go to lunch today? Maybe it'll take your mind off of this B.S."

Lunch? Off-campus? Freshmen aren't allowed to leave the property for lunch, it's an exclusively upperclassmen perk.

It feels like a naughty, rebellious thing to do. But I'm not hurting anyone. Other than some teenage egos, apparently.

"Okay," I reply. "Where are we going?"

"Tacos?"

After all, it is Tuesday.

"Deal. And we have fifth together, how convenient."

I secretly dread the thought of entering that classroom, flaunting our love affair to two girls I consider(ed) my confidants.

I submerge the thought and instead turn my attention to the momentous occasion to take place in two hours' time: an off-campus lunch with my senior boyfriend. How's that for a dream sequence?

I totally get why the off-campus lunch is such a highly coveted experience. You just can't go back. For one, there's an element of freedom that comes with it; a hint of adulthood and responsibility.

I'm the most responsible 14-year-old on the planet, so I have no moral objection (at this point) to participating in the ritual.

We go to this taco place just over the river and through the woods, towards Fashion Island. Having only 35 minutes to get there, eat, and get back safely is a feat of its own accord.

The streets turn into a road race minus the souped-up cars (though some kids have just that—what doting parents they have). Ryan's white Tacoma makes for the chariot of all chariots, complete with its open-air cab and rosary dangling from the rearview mirror.

The equivalent of his white horse.

We snake through the parked cars in the lot by the movie theatre. We called our order in ahead, so we just need to pay and pick up—one of the insider tips for an efficient lunch period off-site.

I wasn't sure how the actual departure from campus would go, i.e. if I would get caught/scolded/punished. Turns out security wasn't super tight this day. A wink from the universe.

As we sit peacefully at the first stoplight before turning right onto Jamboree, Ryan leans over to me and sneaks a quick kiss on my left cheek.

He whispers, "I love you, I just want you to know that."

Best thing he could've said, considering the day's events.

I smile shyly, and rest my left hand on his right thigh. After I gentle squeeze, I return the sentiment.

We scoop up our tacos and skedaddle like a well-oiled machine. Ry has this experience drilled down to a science. I'm quite literally a passenger along for the ride.

Because of our efficiency, we're able to spend precisely eight minutes at Bonita Canyon Sports Park where we enjoy our meal, completing a perfect loop before returning to the school for fifth period.

Ugh, fifth period.

I try as best I can to enjoy my meal and my company, and *live in the moment* as they say, disciplining my mind from wandering to less-pleasant thoughts, like the tawdry tempers of tempestuous teenagers.

How's that for alliteration? Miss T would be so proud.

As the first bell rings, signaling the end of lunch, we pull into the parking lot, sweep past the strolling security guard, and snag a spot in the front row closest to the entry gates that lead to our next class.

Again, it's my lucky day.

"Don't worry, it'll be fine," reassures Ryan, in his best attempt at preparing me for whatever might come next.

Which, truthfully, is anyone's best guess.

Am I being dramatic?

Probably, but I'm willing to grant myself permission at this point, given the circumstances. Can we just revisit how objectively hurtful it is to walk away from someone who is theoretically your *friend* without so much as a courtesy explanation?

It's. Just. Mean.

Ryan and I make our way through the quad and down the corridor to the classroom. It's about two minutes prior to the second bell. Alex and Charlie aren't there yet. Thankfully?

We take our seats—there's no seating chart in this class—on the opposite side of the entrance, strategically so that we can see them when they walk in.

Why do I care so much to see them when they get there? I want to see their reactions, their facial expressions, body language—

any sign that might betray their motives for their miserly behavior not four hours prior.

Just as the bell rings, the gal pals saunter in and take their seats—not before looking directly at me and Ryan. I deadlock eyes with Alex, who averts her gaze and focuses on Ms. Lopez, who hasn't even risen from her desk yet. My eyes float over to Charlie, who turns to Alex upon the conclusion of our staring contest. She whispers something *just* loud enough for the fifteen closest comrades in her proximity, including Ryan and me, to hear.

Apparently they don't leave each other's side. And she thinks she's so independent.

Shock turns to panic turns to sadness turns to rage turns to hatred, over the course of five seconds.

I'm not one to make a scene. I've been taught better. Thank you, Mom and Dad, I get it now.

It takes every molecule of my being to resist fleeing the scene. What I really want to do is cry. In fact, I tear up a little.

Deep breaths.

Ryan doesn't seem to notice, which at this point is okay with me. I'll give him shit for it later.

For now, I just want to get through the next 55 minutes relatively unscathed.

I've never looked at a wall clock so much during a class before. Usually it's my cell phone. But honestly, my eyes started to hurt from the blue light, and I needed something to distract me.

PSA: blue light is bad news. Wear light-filtering glasses, they will save your eyesight. I currently have 20/10 vision and plan to keep it that way.

I digress.

Analog clocks really are fascinating. Somehow, I managed to count the second hand's tick-tocking pretty consistently over the duration of the period.

It just so happened that during this particular class we got lectured on Shakespearean theatre and iambic pentameter. Reminds me of that 90s movie, *10 Things I Hate About You.* In between the ticks and tocks, I've written my own iteration—shocking, I know. Appropriately, this one is a tribute to Ms. Lopez:

I hate the way you talk to me,
And the way you swivel your chair.
I hate the way you type and click,
I hate it when you stare.

I hate your big dumb standing desk
And the way you take your calls.
I hate the way you make me think,
It drives me up a wall.

I hate it, I hate the way you're always right,
I hate it when you lie.
I hate it when you make me laugh,
Even worse when you make me cry.

I hate it when you make a point,
And the fact that you speak in drawl.

But mostly I hate the way I don't hate you,

Not even a little bit,

Not even at all.

Not too shabby for a class period's worth of effort. (Disclaimer: I don't actually hate her. It's simply for effect.) Perhaps more people should abandon their friendships with me; apparently it's great poetry inspo. Not only self-proclaimed—Ryan got a kick out of it. He basically fell out of his chair.

In any case, as fifth period comes to a close, I can't help but anticipate the dynamics that might unfold between friends-turned-foes. Sounds extreme, but in my teenage mind, they might as well be storm troopers.

As the bell rings, everyone rises and starts to gather their belongings. Most people head to the locker rooms to prepare for their sports, Alex and Charlie included. I notice a lingering look from both of them before they abruptly leave the classroom and disappear around the corner.

Classy.

I wonder if they saw me cry.

Probably. Girls tend to be more perceptive about such things. As compared to boys, like my S.O., who is oblivious to my exchange with the Torture Twins.

As soon as they vanish from sight, I turn to Ryan, who's finishing a conversation with Ms. Lopez about his presentation for the next class. It's a monologue from his favorite movie, *The Godfather.* That's a whole other conversation.

Ryan returns to his seat next to me and fiddles away with his backpack. Sometimes the turtle-ness compromises its pack-ability, if that's a word.

FINALLY, we make eye contact as he goes on a tangent about what he's going to wear for his presentation next week, so that he properly captures the essence of Marlon Brando's character.

His words, not mine.

"These guys are New York mafia, so I'm thinking I need to go with a bowler hat and mostly black—"

He stops mid-thought and notices the subtle red blemishes around the corners of my eyes. I don't wear make-up, so there's no ink trail of mascara creating a constellation of sorts down my cheeks—what would be an obvious indication of my state of mind.

But credit to him, he pauses and pursues his line of questioning before arriving at his well-thought-out conclusion:

"Damn, these girls are mean."

Thank you, Captain Obvious.

"That may be true, but that doesn't change how I feel right now," I pander.

"And how is that?"

"Like shit."

I can be so eloquent sometimes.

"I know this is easier said than done, but don't let it get to you. You've got more class than those two combined, you don't need them."

"I know I don't need them," I admit. "It's not about that. It's about their total disregard for my feelings and subsequent sacrifice of our friendship. And their trash talking of me *in front* of me. Classless."

"I love it when you use big words," compliments Ryan. "Sorry, totally off-topic."

He blushes.

Can't be mad at that.

"But babe," he continues, "you gotta remember you can't control that, their behaviors, actions, thoughts, opinions. You gotta focus on what you can control. You taught me that."

He winks one of his wily winks.

He's not wrong.

We gather our books, bags, and bountiful wisdom before evacuating the classroom. We part ways in peace, via a bear hug and biting kisses.

Ryan always manages to make me feel better. Despite our contrasting views on certain topics, like sex and savage tans, he brings me comfort and solace. I need to be more self-sufficient with these things. I'm only 14, I got time.

I unload the day's events to my mom when she picks me up. Jenny had to stay late, so it's just me and Mama.

Her observations?

"I'm sorry you had to go through that, hun. This can be a tough age. Sounds like you're handling it."

Handling it? Hardly.

This is coming from a woman trained and credentialed in the art of the child. Early development is her forte. Not that what I'm experiencing is considered early by definition, but you get the gist: she gets kids.

When we get home, I share a slightly different version with Daddy. I know my audience and what's palatable. Deliveries need to be adapted sometimes; this is just a fact of life. The quicker we learn this, the better our conversations, relationships, and outcomes.

For example, Daddy's version omits Ryan completely. I don't need to go down the rabbit hole of fabled friendships. At least not today.

"I see," he muses. "I don't like your friends."

Such a fatherly thing to say.

"Me neither. They really hurt my feelings."

"People, they are like ships. Sometimes they stay a while at port, and sometimes they leave forever. Not all of them are meant to stay until the end. You learned that lesson today."

I love Daddy's proverbs.

You can bring a horse to water, but you can't make him drink.

That one's my favorite so far.

He's right. As he often is.

Though in this scenario, I do think it's a little extreme to consider my friendship with these girls *over*.

Maybe we just had a bad day?

But then I revisit the feelings of demoralization I endured the entirety of the day, and consider how people that are supposedly my friends purposely inflict such pain and torture.

I could ebb and flow all day on this topic.

And so, I put a pin in that dilemma and focus the rest of my day on spending time with my family.

Meaning, eating a dinner of top sirloin, rice, and salad followed by watching *Jeopardy!*. I love how we all shout out answers at the TV, like it actually makes a difference to the outcome of the show. I find it super gratifying when I get a Final Jeopardy question right. It happens maybe once every month or so, sometimes more often.

I blame the show's writers. People need to be more encouraged; no wonder the ratings are suffering. I will be on that show one day, mark my words.

Especially after a day like today, nothing compares to spending time with family. They (the collective *they*) say it's the small things, how you spend your mornings, how you talk to yourself, what you read, who you share your energy with, what has access to you—that will change your life.

I get it now.

CHAPTER SEVENTEEN
MIC DROP

3 MONTHS (OR WHAT FEELS LIKE 3 YEARS) LATER

Winter turns into spring, which generally equates to milder temperatures and less rain. We've been in a drought over the last few years, and so winter doesn't carry the winteriness we typically experience in Southern California. Because winteriness depends significantly on the geography in question, you can imagine to what extent *winter* actually occurs in our locale during any given year.

What lingers, though, is an icy chill permeating what was once a seemingly-surviving friendship.

I haven't exchanged any meaningful words with Alex and/or Charlie in the elapsed time since the moment of repulsion in front of our lockers.

I say meaningful, because there have been some necessary exchanges in class, such as *Please light the Bunsen Burner* and *Are there any more protractors?*

Hardly the stuff of breakthrough proportions.

It's already April, and there are only eight weeks left of

school. Meaning, eight weeks until Ryan graduates, eight weeks until finals, and five weeks until prom.

Prom has become a sensitive subject.

Prom is the last big event on campus before graduation, Grad Night, and the literal pomp and circumstance that comes with concluding one's high school experience.

Prom is also a date night. Which, roughly translated, means Daddy would not approve.

We've been seeing each other in secret, for all intents and purposes, as far as my dad is concerned. I really don't like keeping something like this from him, but I truly don't believe I'm doing anything wrong. We're not even sleeping together—which, much to Ryan's chagrin, is the biggest sacrifice of our relationship.

Innocent young love, coupled with old soul hearts and melodic musings in the form of poetry—that's all it is.

What's more, my mom is fully aware.

Well, maybe not *fully* aware. If I had to assign a percentage, I'd say she is privy to 95% of all things *Samaryan*.

Obviously, that's significant. I'm not sure if that qualifies as *normal*. Suffice it to say, I recognize I don't exactly meet the standard of normal. I'm okay with that. I have to be if I'm to survive high school without friends.

I literally have no friends.

I sound like a dramatic teenager, which is probably an accurate depiction, too.

Sure, Ryan qualifies. I miss my lady friends. But I respect myself enough where to draw the boundaries.

I digress.

When Ryan first mentions prom, he leads with an assumption,

which he doesn't acknowledge is an assumption.

I hate when people do that; it's one of my pet peeves.

"I know you probably can't go, and it's really important to my mom that I go. Are you okay with that?"

While I appreciate the attempt, I am fuming at the commentary around my ability to participate. We've been dating for months, I'm pretty confident we can figure it out. Why didn't he consider that option?

The lack of effort bothers me. I won't forget that feeling.

My reply, then?

"Well, honey, I'm pretty confident we can make it work. I'll talk to my mom and see what she thinks."

My best attempt to remain calm.

I personally would love to go to prom. And not for the typical status-oriented reasons, i.e. being a freshman at a junior/senior event. That honestly gives me anxiety.

I just really like to dance. When I was a kid, I was a huge hit at weddings, simply because I wouldn't get off the dance floor.

I remember once, the M.C. was clearing the floor for the bouquet toss and called all the "single ladies" to the hardwood. At the time, I didn't know what single ladies meant. I was five, and pre-Beyoncé. I stayed anyways.

And obviously I want to spend time with Ryan, get dressed up, take some photos. Another opportunity to make a memory and create some top-notch IG content while we're at it.

When I mention the idea to Mom, she simply replies, "Maybe you can find a girlfriend to go with you."

A girlfriend … that's a junior or senior.

Ding ding, we have a winner.

Why didn't I think of that? My mom is my hero.

Kay is the answer.

Remember Kay? She is my big sister from my sixth period Bio class. She's the senior who had to take biology because the school she transferred from didn't offer it to freshmen when she was there. Leave it to me to befriend the only senior in our class full of unathletic freshmen, i.e. freshies who don't play sports.

Remember, I take dance. There's a difference.

The next day, I fill Ryan in on the plan.

"I'll just take some photos with Kay to show my dad if he asks," I share.

Now, I'm not *exactly* sure if that's what Mom had in mind. But as far as I'm concerned, optics is just as good as the real thing.

Oh, it's a wonderful digital life.

"This is your mom's idea?" Ryan asks, quizzically.

"It's my mom's idea with a Samantha twist," I correct. "Pretty good, huh?"

"Your mind blows me away, sometimes," Ryan observes.

"I will take that as a compliment," I respond, somewhat in jest but also in seriousness.

"As you should, babe, as you should. Now that that crisis is averted, you just need to find a dress."

I smile, slyly. "My favorite part!"

I'm a closet outfit maker, pun intended. I will make lists upon lists of outfits for each occasion/day of the week. I'm pretty sure I was some kind of stylist i.e. clothing curator in another life. Technically, I *am* a stylist in my current life, I just don't get paid for it.

Maybe that's a future endeavor. I don't think my dad would

go for that. I'll worry about that later.

Today, I'm enjoying our prom prospectus and looking forward to spring break. Every year, my family goes to Palm Desert, past the windmills and just before Joshua Tree. These trips predate me; my parents used to go for weekenders every so often to (physically) distance themselves from their routine.

Over time, it's become more of a family tradition.

(I will low-key celebrate my birthday over spring break. Let's not make a big deal about it, cool thanks.)

Spring break, as well as my birthday, come and go without much fanfare—just the way I like it. It's the last break, notably, where I won't have any upcoming examinations to study for or classes to prep for.

Next year I will take my first AP (i.e. advanced placement) class, World History. Meaning, I will have lots to read this summer. Reading, I don't mind so much.

On my first day of seventh grade, we had a quiz on this book called *Holes*. For some reason, I didn't get the memo that this required reading was due on the first day of class.

Me, the person who always follows directions.

I was mortified. I hate being unprepared. I couldn't bring myself to tell the teacher I majorly screwed up, and thus waded my way through the multiple-choice, true/false, fill-in-the-blank assessment blindly, and without the benefit of a summer's worth of prep. I don't even remember how I did; I must've blocked out the results to save my sanity.

I haven't overlooked a set of instructions since, and don't plan to do so ever again.

Ryan and I decide to go prom dress shopping on a Saturday in May. We figure he's not taking any AP exams, and those that are will probably be studying. Not sure why that matters, but in the moment it feels like sound logic. I think I just don't want to deal with the gossipy gazes of fellow high school savants.

We start at Macy's, because they have the best dress selection. Some girls like to go to these specialty boutiques that quite frankly cost an arm and a leg. I could never spend that kind of money on a prom dress.

I've never met my dad's family. Akram (my *chaachaa*, like the Cuban ballroom dance) came to visit once for a year before I was born. What I know so far is via my dad and photographs from when my mom went to visit in the 80s. In these photos, Shameem (my *chaachii*) always has such elegant outfits. She wears what's called a *salwar kameez*, which consists of loose trousers (the salwar) that narrow at the ankles, accompanied by a tunic top (the kameez). She also wears a *dupatta* or *odani* with her *salwar kameez* to cover her head and shoulders. Women in Bollywood movies tend to sport this kind of ensemble. Mom says when Shameem leaves the house she always has to have her head covered.

I don't wear *salwar kameez*, but I do own a pair of *juttis* which were a gift from Akram and Shameem that Daddy brought back from his last trip. They're basically pointed-toe flats, but with more detailed embellishments in the stitching.

Part of me feels like it's a totally archaic practice for the dude to come along and have input in picking out a dress. Another part of me feels like it's part of the experience we can share and reminisce about when we're old(er).

So, we elect to employ the latter rationale and dive in. We've been "together" about six months now; that feels like a lifetime in high school terms. We've established a level of comfort that comes only with time, a degree of familiarity that only those close to you can experience.

There's also the mythical honeymoon period, where bliss is eternal, until it's not. We're cusping at that point, according to the sage wisdom of CosmoGirl. I'm fully aware of this. I choose to enjoy it for what it is, what it isn't, and what it can be.

Per my own practice, I hit the floor and pull the dresses I like on the hanger that I project will flatter my shape—curvy, yet petite. *Her measurements were 36-25-34*, matching those of Nelly's 90s hit "Ride Wit Me."

As such, I tend to like the flowy-er dresses that offer some shape, but a far cry from the bodycon dresses some of my classmates might buy.

I glance over to Ryan every so often, who has found a throne-like seat outside the dressing room, waiting for the fashion show to begin.

He looks pretty content, if I do say so myself.

He has his (insert app game here) to keep him busy.

Meanwhile, I immerse myself in my own state of shopper's delight.

Until I don't anymore.

As I browse amidst the racks of ruche and ruffle, I catch a glimpse of none other than Alex and Charlie, making their way through the make-up counters of gloss and more gloss.

They love their lip luminizers. Rhianna is definitely onto something.

Charlie clearly senses my stare; you can see it on her face as she lifts her gaze from the glass to my glow. She elbows Alex who, upon contact, abruptly takes notice of our staring contest.

Alex shakes her head and resumes her search for the next top moisturizer.

Oh, hell no.

You know when you've reached a point where you've simply *had enough*?

It's in this moment where I've arrived at this destination, the point of no return.

How did we get here?

We got here because someone made a judgement on how someone else spends their time, and alienated them for it, because it was not aligned with their expectations.

Sounds like a social commentary on modern America. That's a whole other conversation.

Right now, I'm more concerned with my own dignity and sense of self.

And I've just about had it with this forbearing feud.

Without so much as a second thought, I strut towards Ryan with my six or so pre-selected dresses.

"Can you please hold these for me? I need to take care of something right now."

I give him a quick peck before he can offer a rebuttal. I'm not even sure what facial expression he's wearing as I turn on my heels and approach my former friends.

Something tells me it's a look of pride, likely that characteristic smirk he wears after telling a witty joke.

Clad in my high-waisted Lucky jeans and white V-neck, my lucky (ha) outfit and feeling confident AF, I beeline towards the Glossier counter where the girls have since redirected their attention.

I'm not exactly sure what words will reveal themselves just

yet. Shocking, I know. I love words.

As I approach, I'm greeted with mixed looks of awe and audacity, projected accordingly by each damsel equally awashed in dubiousness.

I start with a, "Hello dears, find anything good?"

I try *not* to sound sarcastic, but knowing me, sometimes I just can't help myself.

Each of them mumbles a response I can't make out, and which, quite frankly, I'm hardly interested in.

"Great. In any case, I've approached you today because I have something to say. Your treatment of me over the past few months has been incredibly hurtful and unkind. I don't believe I did anything to deserve it, and if I have, it has not been clearly communicated to me. Walking away in repulsion is not something friends do to each other. If you have issues with who I choose to spend my time with outside of our friendship, that is your problem, not mine. And if you cannot accept my choices, we have no business being friends.

"I have missed you guys, against my better judgement it seems, because I am only human and have amazing memories of us together. However, I will not sacrifice my own happiness for your approval. That's not okay. I would *never* ask or expect that of you, and I respect my own boundaries too much to sacrifice my happiness for anyone, especially you. I don't say this to be mean, I say this because I don't want there to be any gaps in communication or opportunities for misinterpretation. I have no ill will, and quite frankly this monologue has been very therapeutic for me. So thank you. I wish you both the best and I hope you are happy with yourselves and your choices."

That was a mic drop moment if I ever delivered one.

I take a deep breath, smile my signature smile, and slow-curve walk away.

That felt good.

Suddenly I see Ryan lurking behind a display of Michael Kors handbags.

"I heard every word," he blurts. "I'm so proud of you."

Cue the waterworks.

Tears start streaming down my face then and there, subtly silent and without shame. Ryan wraps his arms around me and leads us towards the dressing room where we sit on the plush sofa and just, be.

I'm not sure how Alex and Charlie reacted. In all honesty, I don't care. That moment was for me. Not for anyone else.

No words are exchanged for a few minutes between Ryan and me. We simply exist, together and as one.

"That felt good," I finally squeak. "Now, let's find me a dress."

We spend the rest of the afternoon playing dress-up. Or at least, I do.

We find a white, silky, knee-length dress that has some beading and thin straps that offer enough support for an evening of dancing. It hugs my curves just enough so that I'm not self-conscious but we can still see that I have a shape. Perfect compromise. It also has a surprisingly low back, which is not something I would pick for myself, but it doesn't look half bad. More importantly, I feel comfortable in it.

By the end of the day I'm spent, both literally and figuratively. Who knew shopping for a prom dress could be so eventful?

After I get home, I regale Mama with the day's events. She listens, as only she knows how to, without interference or judgment.

"I'm glad you found your dress. It sounds like it was a great experience to share with Ryan."

Oh, Mama, I hope to one day capture so much feeling in so few words as you do.

CHAPTER EIGHTEEN
THAT CROWD

n due time, Monday is upon us, as the modern-day work week anticipates without disappointment.

I'm wondering, what will this Monday bring?

Given the exchanges of not forty-eight hours earlier, the wake that trails Samantha's sermon could get interesting.

Or so it's a possibility.

It could also be a blip on some remote radar that bears no relevance to the dimension that is Balboa Bay High School.

It's a toss-up.

When I arrive at my locker, I make a concerted effort to lift the lock slowly, in the case that a cruel combative rebuttal is waiting for me.

My imagination.

Nothing happens. I notice no immediate signs of effrontery or destruction.

I float through the day without event. Ryan and I go to lunch at the local juicery down the street, which doesn't require we drive but we do so anyway, because we can.

I enjoy living on the edge. My behavior is so nefarious.

When we get to fifth period, Alex and Charlie are already there, sitting in their seats. I sense they sense our presence as we walk in and take our seats.

No acknowledgement is otherwise given.

I must've made an impact.

Fine by me. Glad to see the message was sent, opened, and read. (And perhaps deleted, which is not my problem.)

I smile, to myself, somewhat satisfactorily. I'm glad I said my peace, my truth. It was one of the hardest things I've ever done.

The risk of losing a friendship is not worth sacrificing myself. And to be clear, I did not do it for a boy. I did it for me.

After class, I take the hard right outside of the drama classroom, down the hall towards Bio class, Ryan at my side.

"Samantha, wait up!" I hear, echoing through the halls of taxidermied fauna.

Lo and behold, the source of the shouting is Charlie. How shocking.

I don't skip a beat.

"Hi Charlie, how are you?"

"Good, Sam, and you? Did you find a dress?"

Ryan's just kind of awkwardly standing there, unsure of whether and/or when to interject.

"I did, thanks for asking." She's not getting anything more than that, as far as I'm concerned.

"Good, I'm glad to hear it. Listen …" she begins. Finally, the meat of the conversation.

"I just wanted to say I hear you. I didn't mean to hurt your feelings. I was talking to my mom and she doesn't like the idea of dating older guys, no offense Ryan."

He kind of shifts his weight and looks at me with an *are you serious?* kind of glance.

Charlie continues, "She doesn't think it's a good idea to associate myself with that crowd. I know that doesn't excuse anything, I just wanted you to know."

Whoa, whoa, whoa. That crowd? Older guys? Her mom?

Ryan can see I'm on the verge of tears and takes that as his cue to swoop in and play the prince. Charlie's mom would probably find that distasteful.

"Thanks for sharing, Charlie. Samantha, can you help me with this assignment before class starts? It could use your editor's eye."

He knows how to abort a failed mission in the classiest of ways.

"Yeah, thanks Charlie," I stutter. "See you later."

"Okay Samantha, chat you later." Charlie nods, faintly smiles, and turns to walk away.

"Does Alex feel the same way?" I manage to squeak out.

"Alex isn't ready to talk, if that helps any," she whispers delicately.

We all know what that means: I'm mad at you and have no intention of speaking to you.

I wish I hadn't asked.

As Charlie leaves, the sobs sweep away any solace I was feeling prior to this encounter with who I would now describe as my former friend.

"You know what the worst part is? Her MOM doesn't like me," I weep. "It's like pre-K all over again."

When I was four, my sister and I went to a pre-school in Palm Desert while our family was on vacation there. Presumably this was to keep us busy and prevent us from spending all of our time at the pool.

I made friends with this girl named Hailey, a cute blonde-haired, blue-eyed cherub of a child, and we became playmates during recess. Things were going great for about a week. We rode the teeter-totter, my favorite, and played on the slide, racing each other to see who could make it down the fastest. It was pure playground bliss.

Then, out of the blue, she came up to me and said, "My mom says I can't be friends with you."

"Why not?" I ask.

"My mom says I can be friends with Chloe, because she's American, and you're not."

Chloe, as it happens, was a similarly a cute, blonde-hair, blue-eyed cherub of a child.

I kept this event to myself until we got home to Newport later that spring, and then cried to my mom about what happened. I remember feeling shame, and not understanding why. Quite an experience for a four-year-old.

It's ten years later and this memory has not left me. Prejudice and stereotypes are still very much alive in our world, and unfortunately are part of what makes us human. However, we can take active measures to reduce their impact and reconfigure our world into one of respect, dignity, and empowerment. It starts with awareness.

Obviously, Hailey's mom didn't get the memo. Unfortunately,

Charlie's mom is employing her own version of bias, conscious or not.

"This world is F-ed up, Sammy," Ryan consoles. "It just goes to show that people will make their judgments with whatever information they have, be it faulty or factual. Parents and kids alike. And as difficult as it is, it shouldn't dictate how you proceed. If you can live with yourself and are happy with the choices you make, by all means, carry on."

"You're so much smarter than me, Ry," I whimper. "Still hurts like a mo-fo though." I laugh, just a little.

"Of course it hurts, babe. You're the most empathetic person I know. You feel more than anyone I've ever met. That's your superpower."

"I'd rather read minds, that would be so much more fun," I jest. Kind of.

Despite the less-than-appealing knowledge I newly acquired, all in all, I am okay. My soul might be (momentarily) crushed, but there are worse things. While the lining might be more of a dull grey than a shiny silver, I'm grateful for the lesson: what others think of me is their choice; what I think of me is my choice.

"I think she's trying to do the right thing," Ryan offers. "The key word here is *try*. In her spot, she's trying to manage her relationship with her parents, you, and herself. And they're all in conflict with each other. That's gotta be rough, I don't envy that. It won't be until she decides only *her* truth matters that she'll come to terms with her feelings."

He is so profound sometimes, it makes me so proud.

"On another note, I wanted to share something with you," pivots Ryan. "I wrote it on Saturday after our little show."

He hands me a folded-up piece of paper, true to form.

It reads:

I can battle my weakness,

I can fight my tears.

I know I can believe in our future.

For in our future,

I see us together

Never leaving each other's side.

Though I fear our separation,

I believe in

Our strength,

Our courage

And our love.

Especially our love—

For our affection is stronger

Than any other aspect

Of our relationship.

I love you—

That's all I need to believe.

I've cried enough today, so I take a deep breath instead, and stifle, "How appropriate."

Thank God he laughs, because as we know, sometimes my humor isn't timed as well as it should be.

"Really, hun, I love it. Couldn't be a better time to express that sentiment. I love you, and I love us. Thank you."

We kiss, as un-PDA-y as we can manage as the sixth period bell alerts us to the conclusion of passing period.

"I'll text you later, babe. Love you," and with another quick peck, Ryan is gone.

How lucky am I to have something that makes saying goodbye so hard?

A Winnie the Pooh original.

It's true, though. It's so easy to get wrapped up in the external chaos that is high school, heartbreak, and the internet. What about world peace? Heck, what about inner peace?

There are times when I don't think the future looks very bright. But then, I think about how happy I can be, how happy I can choose to be.

And so, for now, I can look forward to prom, enhancing my yoga practice, and spending time with Ryan and my family. And the end of the school year, all of five weeks away. That reality is conflicting: it also signals the end of Ryan and my time together on the same campus. He's living at home and will be nearby, but it's not the same. But as I try to do, I appreciate it for what it is, what it was, and what it will be: a memory, full of joy, love, laughter, and hope. I hope to live a life I'm proud of. If I find that I am not, I hope I have the courage to start all over again.

Here's to hoping.

CHAPTER NINETEEN

STARRY NIGHT

The word *prom* is derived from promenade, which is the formal, introductory parading of guests at a party. Proms initially shared more similarities with debutante balls than modern-day school dances. A prom was a relatively simple co-ed banquet that nineteenth century American universities held for each year's graduating class. A burgeoning teenage culture encouraged that proms be held for those younger and younger. By the 1940s, the current rendition of the dance we know today came to exist. In the 1950s, on the heels of a thriving postwar economy, high schools began hosting these events in hotels or at country clubs, as opposed to on campus gymnasiums or cafeterias.

Let us not forget the racial undertones that pervaded the social, political, and economic landscape in the US during this time. In the 1960s and '70s, many once all-white schools that *integrated* (I hate this word, I'm not sure what other verb to use here to explain the conscious blending and consequent sharing of educational resources across racial lines) their classrooms began to hold two proms: one for white students and one for black students. (I always ask the obvious question, what about the brown people? Or the mixed people? Seems like a natural question to me.) I read about a case of Charleston High School in Mississippi, where white parents began organizing invite-only proms for white students in 1970, which happened to be the year black students began attending. In response, black parents organized their own prom for their kids.

Not to hate on Charleston High, but its proms occupied media headlines as recently as 1997, when actor Morgan Freeman (Shawshank!) pledged to pay for the school dance if it agreed to hold one integrated prom. The school actually *refused* and continued holding racially segregated proms until 2008. That was just *barely* a decade ago. And Charleston isn't even the most recent school to desegregate its prom. Wilcox County High School in Abbeville, Georgia, only held their first integrated prom in 2013; the last "whites-only" prom was held that year.

This one is interesting too: an Alabama principal was sued in 1994 for threatening to cancel the prom if interracial couples attended. What world are we living in? Don't even get me started on the gender conversation. Two South Dakota boys became one of the first known same-sex couples to openly attend a prom in 1979, and yet some schools still have anti-gay bans in place. In April 2010, a Mississippi school district canceled its prom rather than allow a student to bring her girlfriend as her date.

Today, at BBHS, we have our own set of promenade standards. These now gala-like parties are accompanied by gala-like amenities, extras, sparkle. We take limos to prom, which is usually hosted at a hotel (like winter formal; only Homecoming is hosted on campus). The guys pay for the tickets and the limo; the girls pay for pictures and dinner. Boutonnières and corsages are exchanged before pictures, usually prior to the "group picture" offsite at some scenic location like Inspiration Point overlooking the ocean or someone's fancy, picturesque backyard. Let's not forget the "prom-posal," the gesture of all gestures to accompany the simple question: "Will you go to prom with me?" I've seen billboards, flight patterns, notes on cars, intercom poetry during Monday morning announcements. I'm sure there's more I'm failing to recount.

The pressure and anxiety that accompanies these gestures, or lack thereof, is intense, especially for hormone-driven teens. I think of classic movies like *She's All That*, *Never Been Kissed* and *Mean Girls* that first started popularizing the modern-day mainstays associated with the prom ritual; while entertaining, they certainly set expectations amongst the impressionable high school crowd for what a prom experience should (could?) be. It's like what Disney did with fairytales: princesses locked away in a metaphorical (sometimes literal) version of a tower by a scheming third party somehow managing to be rescued by their rendition of Prince Charming. These expectations are dangerous, and certainly not one size fits all.

For example, Ryan wrote a poem and asked me, *verbally*, to the dance. What a concept that is. Given our relationship, I would hardly expect him to perform some grandiose gesture that does nothing but show me how creative he can be. He already does that with his poetry, so I ask, what's the point? I *have* heard of seniors, other seniors, asking underclassmen because they think they're hot and might get lucky, and therefore go to great lengths to craft impressive intimations to demonstrate their dominance. This is what I would call peacocking at its finest. Peacocking is just what it sounds like: the behavior of a male peacock, strutting around, showing off his beautiful feathers and fair-weather charm.

Then there's the whole Prom King/Prom Queen nomination and voting process, the token theme (ours is "Starry Night," as in Vincent Van Gogh's classical painting)—not to mention organizing the entire itinerary from the pictures to the dinner to the actual dance to the after party. So many logistics to coordinate.

I don't feel entitled or privileged about going to the dance.

After all, it's just a dance. I have enough anxiety to manage what with the angsty and asinine attitudes of my once-*amies*. It seems like during every break, transition, and lunch period a new pairing is announced and applauded by the masses, comparable to the hurrahs in the wake of a groom and bride sharing their first kiss at the altar. The whole prom thing feels like a dress rehearsal for the "Big Day." So much pressure! Most of us are still legally considered children. Notwithstanding cultural norms across various nations, tribes, and other units of community, at this point in time I'd like to focus on my education and setting myself up for academic success. I think my parents would agree with that. True, I have a doting boyfriend—who, for the record, I have no intention of marrying. I'm not even sure I want to get married. But I digress.

I'm personally looking forward to the actual dancing part. I could do without the accessory hoopla. Finding the dress so far has been the best part, aside from the actual shopping experience itself.

The day arrives, somewhat apathetically. Most girls spend the morning at the hair and/or nail salon, primping and pampering their bags of bones with the goal of achieving prom-look-perfection— myself included. I'm not sure where this comes from, it has to be some innate, biological preference. Perhaps it's part of a woman's social inclination to attract a mate and in the process enjoy the company of other women in her circle. Perhaps it's a testament to the experience economy we're so immersed in. Perhaps it's a combination of both.

In any case, Mama, being the saint that she is, arranges to spend her day chauffeuring me between a hair and make-up appointment at the local School of Cosmetology, the nail salon, and the flower shop to pick up Ryan's boutonnière. Per societal norms, Ryan and I hotly debated the color of the flower, the color of the ribbon, the size, giving probably unnecessary attention to every minute detail. (By debate, I mean Ryan deferred to my judgement.)

We did it for the 'gram.

We decided on a red centerpiece, a rose, with baby blue ribbon to match my shawl-scarf-wrap. Since my dress is white, I insisted on a pop of color. And no, my dress does not by any means resemble a wedding dress.

As much as he shies away from the hubbub of these traditions, Ryan also enjoys the participation, the active engagement. He's a social butterfly, that one.

He texts me around 8 a.m. on this morning.

Are you ready for the ball?

While I appreciate the cheesiness of the Cinderella subtext, the remaining plotlines of the folktale do not apply. I am no persecuted heroine—or am I? Given my recent (less than) repartee and subsequent demotion in the matriarch's view, such a description bears the slightest bit of resemblance. An ironic and unintentional application, I'm sure. Even Ryan isn't *that* good. At least I'm not a victim of the Salem witch trials. History has not been kind to anomalous women.

I reply,

just waiting on my fairy godmother
to do her magic

I could have been persecuted for this statement in 1692.

Today's equivalent: beauticians and their blow dryers.

That's some dark magic.

I forgo yoga today and decide to write in my journal, to document my joy, my glee, my hesitation, my fear. I'm nervous to spend the evening with people—older people—I don't know at all, who probably have formulated their own opinions of me weeks ago.

The easy freshman. Plain and simple. I doubt the analysis

extends beyond these three words, as these three words *say it all*. From what Ryan has told me, we are in a group of 22, or 11 couples, with whom he's not the closest but has some casual relationships, as he calls them. The guy who took the lead in organizing the group, Vick, happens to be the older brother of one of my classmates. Any little bit of familiarity adds comfort.

The ritual run-of-show commences at 5 p.m., when we meet at Inspiration Point for pictures and our ride, the Hummer stretch limo. I realize how obnoxious this sounds; this is part of the experience, as I understand it. The responsible rationale is such transportation limits the incidence of drunk driving. The first limo I took was for my friend's eleventh birthday when we went to Disneyland, eight of us kids and her mom and friend. Different circumstances, same vehicle.

The limo takes us to our first stop: dinner. Followed by the dance, and finally, the after party. The after party is hosted at Vick's house. Ryan has planned to leave his car at Vick's prior to pictures so he can take me home afterwards. If all goes according to the pre-planned timeline, I should be home by midnight.

I have my GPS turned on so that Mama will know where I and my cell phone are at all times. Daddy is aware that today is the day, and is attuned to as many details as he cares to remember, aside from the tiny deviation as to my companion for the night. Photographic evidence will be secured to support our claims. Kay, gracious creature that she is, is party to our plan.

"I'm happy to help," she giggles. "You're my little sister, of course I'll help you." I promise to repay her with gratitude and something tangible once I figure out what that is. I wish she was in our prom group.

I write about the guilt I feel for not sharing this life event with someone so close to me, but if I did, there would be no event to speak of. I rationalize some things are best kept secret, behind a boundary. While Daddy's intentions are to protect me, I need to protect myself. And sometimes, that means unsanctioned exploration.

By 10 a.m., I've had enough time to introspect and get ready for my hair appointment at 11 a.m. I hope my updo stays intact, at least until pictures.

I change into lululemon joggers and a zip-up hoodie, so when it's time to get ready I'm not pulling a shirt over my head and risking the ruin of my hairstyle. It's in the mid-60s this morning so I don't worry about overheating. I sweat early and often; thank you, Indian circulatory system.

When we get to the hair/make-up place, it's teeming with teen girls prepping for their nights out. I don't recognize anyone, I gather because prom in our school district is a junior/senior event; and I'm a measly freshman with only two upperclassmen friends, one of whom also happens to be my boyfriend.

It's lonely sometimes, being in a relationship with an older guy. I think some of it is in my head—that his peers don't like me, that they think I'm too young and naïve and have no vested interest in a relationship other than the PR that comes with dating an older man on a high school campus. Though there are kernels of truth in these considerations. It's my choice, and I accept the terms. I could do a better job calling on my own sense of courage rather than living in the self-cast shadows of teen torture.

"How do you want your hair, hunny?" asks Philipe, my stylist and new favorite person. His Brazilian accent and hot pink leather pants light up my central occipital lobe.

I pull out my phone and scroll through saved posts on my Instagram to give him an idea of what I'd like. It's the real-world application of show, not tell. My English teacher would be so proud.

"Definitely up and off my neck, but not tight like a ballerina bun. I like some strands loose in the front to frame my face, kind of like this. Does that make sense?"

Philipe regards my phone with a furrowed brow and concurrent twinkle in his eye, and stance reminiscent of the bend-and-snap.

"I got you, girl," he announces, "now, watch me work!"

I cannot help but smile.

While Philipe sections my hair, he prompts the typical questions one might expect from a hair stylist on the morning of prom.

"What school do you go to? Who's your date? Ohhhhh, a senior … I bet the girls hate you!" (Obviously, more an observation than a question.) "What color is your dress? Your shoes? Your purse? Where are you going for dinner? Don't forget to bring flip-flops to the afterparty!"

While I appreciate a good chit-chat session, my anxiety over the upcoming evening is beginning to amplify. I think Philipe picks up on this, as I slide into a cone of silence and stare off into oblivion, as I usually do when I get stressed out. Or sometimes hangry.

Bless his heart, because in less than an hour, using nothing more than a curling iron and a few hair clips, he unveils his masterpiece.

When he turns my chair towards the mirror, I see a billowing cascade of curls, loosely looped, haloed around my head like a wreath worn by angels. I see the two strands, not too thick, tucked behind my ears and parted just off-center as per my personal preference.

It looks beautiful.

"What do you think?" he asks, more singing than an actual question.

"I think you best be spending your time on the likes of

Angelina Jolie instead of prepping me for prom!"

"How old are you?"

I know where this is going. "Fourteen, why?" I ask, not because I don't know the spectrum of potential answers, but because I'm curious more than anything. Sometimes people can surprise you.

"You sound like Betty White from *The Golden Girls*," he comments. I remind him of a character from an 80s sitcom living the joys and angst of their golden years. Sounds about right.

He follows it up with, "I love it!"

That's probably the best compliment my old soul has ever received.

I grin—no, beam—a victorious visage of satisfaction.

See! I don't need you. My mind envisions a collective *you* as anyone who doesn't support all that is and will be the collective *me*.

"Now, we do the make-up," declares Philipe. "Tell me what you like. Light? Dark? Angel? Devil? Fairy princess? Devilish vixen?"

Another instance of dualities I hadn't yet thought of.

"Well," I think aloud, "can we do a little of both? Like, a fairy princess with devilish charm?"

I pause briefly to wonder if this analogy resonates to any degree whatsoever. After a moment of some brain scanning of his mental archival database of make-up looks, Philipe nearly salutes in attention and chants, "Si! I got you!"

He whips out a fantastic display of cosmetic perfection: a black, sequin-topped vanity case, embroidered with *PIP*, which I can only assume to be his initials, unless he has a healthy appreciation for one of Charles Dickens's most well-known protagonists. He has every type of wand, brush, and curler you could ever imagine, each instrument a stately black hue. I sense a theme. I can't imagine each of these beauty tools has a name. It makes me feel like Frenchie, *Grease*'s token beauty school dropout; the closest I will ever get to beauty school is in this moment, being primped and pampered by Philipe, a stellar student with tremendous potential.

It takes Philipe literally fifteen minutes to paint his canvas that is my post-pubescent face. I'm one of those lucky girls who doesn't break out. I'll get one pimple when I get my period, but other than that, my skin is clear. It's the melanin, courtesy of Papa Selim, which also allows me to keep some version of a bronzy glow year-round. This is Southern California, after all.

Philipe has chosen what I can only describe as a golden glow, complete with a sultry smokey eye that not too sexy— less midnight, more twilight. My hazel eyes pop, the shadows accenting the green that frames my pupils. Outlined in blackest-black liquid eyeliner, the shape of my eyes are exaggerated to look like cat eyes, which, to my surprise, works. My lips wear a subtle nude color, matte yet shiny. Topped off with a dusty rose cheek, the fairy princess with devilish charm is ready for her version of a ball.

The moment I catch my own eyes in the mirror, I gasp, ever so slightly.

That's me.

Another dimension of me.

Just then, I feel my phone buzz in the side pocket of my yoga pants, the ones that are stitched in the lining and hug against the outside of your thigh.

How's it going? Are you beautiful yet?

I'm not a person that likes to take selfies. In fact I despise it. If I were, I would send him a neck-up shot with a pouty face, half-winking half-scowling.

But since I'm not, I settle for the retort:

just shaking what my mama gave me 

Which in no way actually answers the original question. This is on purpose. It makes me laugh and makes him suffer. At least, I'd like to think so.

Mama's ears must've been burning, because just then she walks into the salon and sees me, her first-born, her ruler breaker of an offspring. She's carrying a Jamba Juice smoothie for me, ever the mama bear.

"Honey, you look wonderful," she remarks, choking back tears in the most subtle way.

"Thank you, Mama," I accept, blushing and a tad emotional. "Are you ready to go? I think we're pretty much done, right Philipe?"

"Aye!" agrees Philipe. "My work here is done. Now go have good time with the boyfriend. Make sure he gives you good time." He half-hugs me with his free hand, the one not holding the mascara wand, to ensure my look isn't compromised even before leaving the salon.

"Thank you, Philipe! I'm so appreciative," I say gratefully, while handing him some cash from my side pocket on the other side of my yoga pants. He takes it between his hands, as if in a sign of prayer.

I will later learn that Philipe uses his cash tips to send to his mom in Mexico to help her pay their bills and housing.

Our next stop is the flower shop to pick up Ryan's boutonnière. I learn they all basically look the same, with variance depending on color, and obvious upgrades correlated with how much you spend. Ryan's boutonnière has three mini red roses, set upon a bed of baby's breath and pulled together by an ever-so-light blue ribbon. Traces of wedding wingdings recur yet again.

By the time we get home, it's close to 2 p.m. In that time, I take my seat on my favorite couch and, without dislodging the carefully tucked wispies, recline delicately yet nimbly, like a ragdoll propped on her proportionally-sized rocking chair. We'll leave for pictures around 4:30 p.m.

By 4 o'clock, I'm in my room, bathing myself in deodorant and perfume. Per my organizational inclinations, my dress, shoes, shawl, purse, and jewelry are all laid out and ready to be adorned. My shoes—or rather, platformed prisms—can essentially be described as the chunky-heel equivalent of Cinderella's glass slippers. (This irony is not lost on me.) My purse, taut white leather with sequins, fits neatly over my shoulder, large enough to hold my student ID, cash, house key, and emergency credit card from Mama. My mom got me this choker, made of delicate wire and white flowers, also metallic. They glimmer, like the sequins, when the light catches. When taken together, my ensemble showcases the fairy princess in me, a youthful exuberance with a purposeful nod to tradition. Philipe nailed it.

I regard myself in my full-length mirror. This is the first time that I have willfully wardrobed my corps in such glamorous attire. Well, aside from those times Alex, Charlie and I would try on special occasion dresses in Bloomingdale's simply for the thrill of it, and document our whimsical bliss using a polaroid camera. (Not our iPhones, that would be a blackmailer's dream.) Even in these instances, we didn't experience the pinnacle of party perfection.

My march down memory lane makes me miss them in this moment. I allow myself a moment to brood, then, positive peach that I am, take a deep breath and give myself an extra moment to enjoy myself. *You're going to the prom. You love to dance. You're spending an evening with Ryan, a boy that you love. Enjoy that.*

Just before 5 p.m., Mom and I pull up to the curb alongside Ocean Ave., across the street from Inspiration Point where our group pictures will take place. We're lucky to get a spot so close; limos parallel park alongside this and tandem alleys as their requisite prom-goers hover along the sidewalk, hoping to capture the most IG-optimized image. I'm realizing this is one of the more popular spots to capture these pre-prom moments. Real estate is a hot commodity.

I get it, though—the view is stunning. Just beyond the bluffs that hang over Big Corona's state beach is the Wedge, a jetty that juts out from the curvy coastline and bisects the city into pieces, the south side being Balboa Peninsula, the north side being Corona del Mar. The sun is still a few hours away from setting, and floats like a suspended trapeze performer just above the horizon. Boats, from Duffys to tugs to superyachts, glide effortlessly across the channel waters at or slightly above the harbor's five-knot, no-wake speed limit.

There's a driveway that begins at the lip of the sidewalk and serpentines through five homes that are built into the side of the cliff. When you look down from their balconies, all you see is ocean with a series of sea stacks poking up through the surface from the ocean floor. The vistas are incomparable; architecture like this is artwork. Either you're a person who appreciates the scenic space created so much you aspire to or do live in it, *or* you appreciate it from afar. There really is no happy medium.

I see Ryan, futzing around with his white necktie as he gazes out over the ocean, looking rather serene. In all honesty he's probably checking out the surf. He's still cute, though.

We decided he would wear all black—jacket, shirt, and pants—with a white tie, capped off with black dress shoes. His blonde tidy mop of a hairstyle, slicked back with pomade, shines in the setting sun. His sophisticated ensemble cannot be overstated.

After a steady fifteen seconds, he turns around and sees me. I shake my head in embarrassment and blush a little as he reacts with a dramatized *be-still-my-heart* expression. How he knows the precise placement of my bashful buttons.

As he approaches me, I see his parents appear from beyond a group of other parents, likely gushing about their pending-graduation prodigy. I don't think they like me very much, mostly because I'm the girl who stole their son's heart. An act of theft impermissible to a parent. It's not personal. At least, I don't think it is.

"You look stunning," Ryan compliments as he approaches me and my mom. He's carrying what I can only assume to be my corsage. "Hello, Mrs. Selim," he follows up with an acknowledgement of my mom.

"Hello, Ryan," Mama greets, "I don't think I've seen you without boardshorts," she muses. "You are very handsome."

Ryan turns a mild shade of crimson as he wraps his arm around my shawl-covered shoulders while simultaneously removing the floral wristlet from its box.

"This is for you," he whispers, like it's some kind of surprise.

"I am in a state of shock!" I sarcastically swoon. "I had no idea you were planning on getting me a corsage."

"You're so cute, Sam," he chides sardonically. "Just put it on, already."

I let him take my freshly manicured hand and slide on the matching corsage—red roses, blue ribbon. He does this as his parents approach, leisurely making their way over with no sense of urgency whatsoever. Message sent.

"Happy Prom Night!" Mr. Prince sings.

"Beautiful dress, Samantha," Mrs. Prince offers.

"This is my mom, Jane," I interject their superficiality with some substance. "Mama, these are Ryan's parents, Mr. and Mrs. Prince."

"Please call us John and Denise," Mrs. Prince replies. "It's lovely to meet you, Jane. Samantha is a treasure, we are very fond of her."

Lies.

My mom being who she is and sensing my discomfort, suggests Ryan and I mingle with the other kids while the adults find their prime picture-taking positions.

We scamper off, leaving the Princes and Mama to their own devices.

"I don't think your parents like me very much," I divulge. "They didn't even try to hide it."

"They're just being protective," he rationalizes. "Don't hold it against them, they don't know any better."

Like *that* makes it okay. I archive that summation to explore at a later date. For now, it's time for the night to commence.

It isn't as awkward as I'd projected, meeting the rest of our prom party. Most people are nice to my face, mature enough to reserve judgement in its physical form. Others, not so much. It's the law of human behavior: plotted on a spectrum, with a majority demonstrating what can be considered moderate behavior, and other less frequently occurring extreme behavior sprinkled in, superimposed on a bell curve.

We exchange pleasantries, talk about the tried and true default intro topics: weather, pop culture, summer plans. After pictures and halfway through the limo ride, we have exhausted them thoroughly. I mostly just talk to Ryan the whole time.

I try to put on a brave face for him. As excited as I am to be there, I feel aloof, excluded, a regular Greaser in a group full of Socs—the quintessential Outsider. It's the perfect blend of adrenaline and serotonin, mixed with Xanax to manage the anxiety.

At dinner, I sit on the end so I don't have a neighbor to my right, which at least halves the amount of conversation I'm expected to make.

Thankfully, Ryan is a gold-medal conversationalist, and doesn't seem to notice my sudden shyness. A double-edged sword; it would be nice if he did notice. I am, after all, his date, his girlfriend, his partner.

I decide to save this conversation for later.

Because the venue for the dance is the Disneyland Hotel, our group has dinner at the House of Blues in Downtown Disney. I appreciate the strategery; proximity is important when planning a ritual run-of-show.

While at dinner, Ryan does this thing where he puts his hand in the middle of my back and strokes it as we're eating and chatting with our table. Now, I'm not a prude per se, but I don't particularly agree that this is the time and place for skin-on-skin contact, no matter how PG the gesture might be. Maybe I'm overreacting, maybe I'm not as *mature* as the seventeen and eighteen-year-olds we're sharing our evening with. However, I don't see other dudes feeling the need to exert their male machismo at the dinner table.

I excuse myself to the restroom, as I don't want to make a

scene.

When I come back, he resumes his stroking session.

"Ry," I whisper, "can you stop doing that?"

"Doing what?" he's utterly confused.

"Rubbing my back like you're marinating a steak," I say in hopes the joke will ease the underlying message of the delivery, which is: please stop touching me.

It doesn't.

He retracts his hand like he's trying to escape a snake pit.

"Sorry," he winces, more embarrassed than apologetic. Who is this person?

"No worries, babe," I lightly reply. "No big deal."

He and I both know it's not *no big deal*, we're just not sure what size of the deal just yet.

I take his hand in mine, again hoping to quell the quandary we've found ourselves in. That seems to help. He smiles as I rest my head on his shoulder, our version of a truce.

We're probably at the dance for no more than two hours, a singular stop on the itinerary that is this ritual run-of-show. An irony, that the activity around which this whole tradition is based only earns a fraction of dedicated participation. The after-party will see the most attention.

And a Starry Night it is. While I don't see many attributions to Van Gogh's work, there's lots of black and sparkle, which I suppose is a nod to the work's color palette. At times, because of the black on black, Ryan looks like a floating head from the Haunted House attraction at Disneyland. The dance floor, a perfect square, twenty feet by twenty feet, flanked by cocktail high-tops and seventy-two-inch banquet rounds seating ten each, supports the traffic of a sleepy 405 freeway. EDM music blares from speakers to this near-empty room. Most of the partygoers loiter in the entryways, chatting with their friends and taking videos for their social media stories. I would think dancing and other purposeful activities might offer better content.

While at the dance, we take our couples' photos, solo photos (to add to the photographic support of our narrative for the evening) and photos with Kay. She looks beautiful, wearing a vintage-type black dress with petticoat skirt and off-the-shoulder sleeves. I'm not even sure who her date is. Does that make me a bad friend?

"What do you think?" I ask Ryan, intentionally vague and in broad application, hoping to get a sense of where his head is. He's been relatively quiet the past hour, even for him. I'd like to know why.

"It's cool," he replies. "I thought there would be … I don't know … more? It seems kinda anticlimatic."

"Anticlimactic, babe," I correct. I can't help myself. "Climatic refers to weather, climactic refers to climax, which I assume if what you're referring to."

He looks at me like I'm high.

"What! I didn't make it up. I'm just the messenger."

"You've had a lot of messages to relay today …" his voice trails off.

Oh no, he didn't.

"What is that supposed to mean?" I try not to sound defensive, but quite frankly, I feel the need to be defensive.

"Nothing," he dismisses. "Let's go dance, shall we, Sam?"

I hate when he dips out of conversations like that. Classic male avoidance.

Ryan grabs my left hand in his right, and beelines to the dancefloor, dodging idling revelers, like he's executing consecutive cutbacks on a reef break wave. I don't feel jerked around or anything, though I do question his determination.

As I mentioned before, I like dancing, a lot. I started taking ballet lessons when I was five years old, and never really lost the urge. I like choreography, the intent behind the movement, the anticipation of what comes next. Dancing is yet another illustration of my propensity for planning, an appreciation for the sanctity of a script in whatever form, be it words or rhythm. Though, it's not to say I don't enjoy a good improv. Sometimes Mama and I will host our own dance parties in the kitchen, blasting her favorites like Garth Brooks and Toby Keith (which I admittedly find to be musically magical myself). We choreograph our own two-person line dancing routines and do-si-do around the kitchen island like it's a bonfire at a pep rally for the rivalry football game. One night around 8 p.m., my brother came home and said he could hear the music from the street. He said it sounded like a rock country house party. Proud moment for Mama and me, two females under 5'5" moving and grooving to their heart's content.

The song selection at prom doesn't include a lot of country music, limiting the amount of stomping and square stepping. I gather it's a preventative measure and out of safety concerns. They do play the Cupid Shuffle, a favorite of mine. I can't believe that dance has been around for over a decade.

Ryan and I don't speak much while we dance, if you could call it dancing. We manage to get on the dancefloor just as the slow dance music comes on, a.k.a. Ed Sheeran. Slow dancing isn't really dancing at all; it's more like swaying. At least it's an accessible type of dance that even the most uncoordinated of people can attempt with high percentages of success.

"Are we okay, Ry?" I interrupt the elegance of an Ed Sheeran original with my inane question. I'd liken it to the equivalent of self-flagellation, a masochistic meme.

"Of course," Ryan replies, obviously thinking better of going down the rabbit hole of whether we're okay. How are we defining *okay* anyway? I'm not even sure how I'm defining it.

"Are you having fun?" I continue. Just put me out of my misery already. How are we defining *fun*? I could play this existential game all day, if only in my own mind.

"Yeah, are you?"

Death by a chilled staccato of a conversation.

"It's cool," I manage. "It's nice to see everyone dressed up nice."

And that's the end of that conversation.

We float a little while longer on the dancefloor, until Vick comes around to corral the group to depart for the after party.

There's a dessert bar by the exit where everyone hovers before finding their respective ways to their rides. On this fifteen-foot-long table sit sweet and savory treats from every category of confection: cakes, chocolates, danishes, donuts, pies, cookies, skewered fruits for the gluten-free community—you name it. At either end of the table are goodie bags for carrying your selective stash. I scoop up what's left of the See's butterscotch and Bordeaux squares—at least a dozen each—into my goodie bag and shuffle away like a sweet-toothed bank bandit hoarding her day's heist. Sweet Sally could be my criminal code name.

That behavior gets a laugh out of Ryan, who's still eyeing the red velvet cupcakes while I'm well beyond earshot and savoring my first butterscotch square of the night on a bench near the car port on the far side of the entryway. A butterscotch square is basically brown sugar coated in milk chocolate—a gift from the candy-making gods.

I see Ryan eventually, and with great amounts of pep, select that red velvet cupcake with his left hand, grab a cocktail napkin with his right hand, and dart away from the table, a wake of guilt trailing his Sperry dress shoes.

He approaches me with his loot in hand.

"Don't feel guilty, babe. I look like I just ransacked the chocolate shop at Fashion Island," I joke. "One cupcake is a mere morsel compared to the job I just went on."

He laughs, thankfully. "I love you, Sam. Who says that?"

Suddenly I feel sheepish and unworthy. I don't think this is his intention, but nonetheless, here we are. I must have cultivated the whole spectrum of human emotion throughout the course of this one evening. That can't be healthy. What is going on? With me? With *us*?

"Look," I interrupt my own thoughts, "there's our limo. Shall we?"

"We shall," Ryan stuffs the rest of his cupcake in his mouth so that he sounds like he's trying to speak while underwater. A shining example of his boyish charm.

We're the first ones in the limo, and make our way towards the back so that the stragglers don't have to crawl over our knees, which is basically the equivalent of a set-up for an ill-fated obstacle course. It's hard enough maneuvering in these shoes on even asphalt, let alone with varying barriers. I did remember to bring flip-flops, thank you Philipe!

I nestle my head on Ryan's shoulder. I can safely say we are both tired from the evening's events; it's literally a full-day affair, at least for those of us who use the early part to beautify ourselves. It looks like most people feel the same way, though I believe this is the *power nap* segment before the real party begins. The real party which I choose to not be a part of, preferring to go to sleep in my matching set of Victoria's Secret leopard print pajamas and baby doll to snuggle with. Yes, I sleep with a doll. Ryan sleeps with a Snoopy so there's no judgement in this relationship.

We conclude this leg of the night at Vick's house, after a thirty or so minute car ride back to the coast. We disembark the Hummer and make our way inside the palatial estate (not an exaggeration). Vick's parents have created quite a space for the after-party-participants—an array of food from In-N-Out on the dry bar begs to be consumed, a video gaming station is prepped and ready to go in the family room, and the pool deck hosts unicorn floats and fun noodles for anyone who wishes to partake in a late-night swim. While enticing, I'm ready for this day/night to be over.

Ryan feels the same. He whispers, "Are you ready to go? My car is here and I can take you home."

Duh, Ryan, we planned this already.

"Sure, we can go," I reply, deciding it's not worth the effort to correct his memory. So far it hasn't worked in my favor, anyway. "We can stay longer if you like to. I don't have to be home until midnight." How considerate am I, affording some choice, especially after the evening we've had.

He considers this option, then answers, "No, I'm tired, let's get going."

Good choice.

We set off to find Vick and say our goodnight's in the process. Everyone is cordial and friendly, and some are already drunk from the nips they had in their purses in the limo. How did I miss that?

Ryan spots Vick and thanks him for his efforts coordinating the evening's festivities.

And then, the kicker.

"I gotta take Sam home, her mom's expecting her home soon, but we had a great time and enjoyed hanging out with everyone tonight."

What. the. Hell.

One of my biggest pet peeves is showmanship, defined here as a performance intended to convey a reality that isn't truth for the purposes of approval, respect. Ryan will deny it, but he has a tendency to perform when the circumstances suit him, at the expense of whomever needs to be the sacrificial lamb, including, most obviously, me.

Does it hurt me, in all senses of the word, to be viewed as someone who needs to go home early because her mother is expecting her, likely because she's younger and therefore has a different set of expectations to abide by? I do have a different set of expectations, but not for the reasons that are expressed on the surface, in conversation. I digress.

The error here is the lack of truth, the misnomer, the excusatory nature of the claims made; that is the fallacy. An intrinsic contradiction in the foundation of which we share ourselves, Ryan and I, or so I had come to believe. That's what's bothering me, the violation of truth.

Joke's on me.

I've heard/read/learned that there's a point in every relationship where the honeymoon period ends and reality sets in. Some say it's six months, some say a year, depending on a plethora of variables. In summary, the *honeymood* (I made that one up) lifts when the relationship no longer feels fresh and exciting, and you're no longer constantly learning new things about each other or having first times together.

Is our honeymood over, all but ten months in? Even if it is, how do we move forward?

I'm spinning in these moments as we walk towards Ryan's Tacoma and set the course towards my house: down Jamboree, right on PCH, right onto the Newport Blvd offramp, and cruising a couple of miles. It's maybe a fifteen-minute ride at best given the time of night, and almost eleven. I told my mom I'd be home by (or rather, that my curfew is) midnight. I'm stewing in my own witch's brew of resentment and irritation. And Ryan has no idea, clearly, from the smirk slapped across his face.

"What a fun night," Ryan proclaims. "Thank you for being an amazing date. I'm so grateful to have you." He takes my left hand to his lips and kisses it surely and softly, while his other hand flippantly guides the steering wheel. He's distracted by his own immersion into the moment. I feel so safe.

"Yeah," I agree, "it was fun."

And then, I can't resist.

"… Until I felt like an escort rather than your girlfriend."

He looks genuinely surprised.

"Um, you were my escort?"

Oh, so we're going down that road.

"I mean escort, in the sense of paid service."

He looks at me like I have six heads.

"For example," I continue, "at dinner you were stroking my back pretty suggestively. And that's cool when we're alone and in private. But out with our classmates … honestly, I felt a little cheap."

He doesn't say a word, keeping an eye on the road and just, drives.

"And," I take his silence for tacit compliance, "when you told Vick you had to get me home, when you wanted to go home, too, I felt like you deliberately made me the bad guy. That didn't feel good either."

We drive in silence for a few blocks before Ryan breaks the stone-cold quiet.

"I'm sorry I made you feel that way," he begins. "I didn't

realize I was doing that. I apologize." He doesn't look at me as he says this, his eyes remain fixed on the asphalt ahead.

"I appreciate that," I acknowledge. At least he's listening. "Do you get why it made me feel bad?"

"Honestly, Sam, it doesn't seem like a big deal to me."

Ouch, that one hurt.

"I think I should be allowed to touch my girlfriend whenever I feel like it," he justifies, "and why does it even matter what reason I used to leave the party? We were leaving anyway, so who cares …"

I'm fuming now, feeling my face heat up like an oversized French press. The touching-the-girlfriend thing I'll deal with later. For now, I focus on the clear effrontery regarding our exit.

"Exactly!" I'm nearly shouting. "If it doesn't matter, why didn't you tell him the *truth*?"

We're approaching my street now. Ryan turns off the main road to the side street across the way from my house, parks the car, and turns off the engine.

"Why are you so obsessed with the truth? Who even cares *why*? You're getting worked up over nothing."

Belittling doesn't even begin to describe the tone of this boy's paltry excuse for an apology. In fact, it turned into an accusation, that somehow this conversation and the road we're on is *my* fault. He must've left his sense of ownership and accountability at Vick's house.

"Because," I attempt, blinking back tears, "if you can't be honest with yourself, how will you ever be honest with me?"

Self-care 101, honey. It's like those emergency instruction videos on airplanes: you first secure your own oxygen mask before helping others around you; if you don't put yourself in a position to be available to help others, you're setting yourself up for failure.

I sit for a few seconds, practicing my breathing and collecting my wits. Then, I grab my purse, my shoes, and my candy bag before opening the car door and removing myself physically from this antagonistic altercation.

I turn around and face Ryan, who's still sitting behind the wheel, tie untied, top button unbuttoned, looking cute as ever, yet at the same time, like a villain in a teeny-bopper movie.

"I hope you enjoyed your evening. Thank you for the ride. Have a good night," I calmly excuse myself and make my way towards my house. I'm so grateful for the flip-flops right about now, my feet started to blister from the platforms.

He doesn't come after me, which is just as well. I don't have anything further to say, to explain. I'm not in the business of beating dead horses.

Mama is awake when I walk in. She's watching her Turner Classic Movies, curating the potpourri scent of a bowl of popcorn accentuated by burning incense—jasmine, I think it is. She hears me fussing with the lock, which is testing my patience given my recent exchange, not to mention the ark-full of items I'm holding. She greets me at the door and offloads my cargo, second-nature as it is to her.

"Sammy, honey, how was your night?" she asks as she kisses me on the forehead. As she steps back to look at me, she immediately notices my tear-stained expression and accompanying frown.

"Did something happen?"

She knows me so well.

"We just got in an argument," I sniff, assuming the parties involved in the descriptive *we* are implied.

"Oh dear," she sighs as she rubs my shoulders and leads me to the swivel chair she spends her late TV-watching nights in. "What happened, honey?"

"He's just being a stupid boy," I pout, ever the eloquent angry person. "He did the thing where he projects his own securities on me, and when I called him out on it, he shut down and blamed me for being upset. Men are the worst," I huff as I dry my eyes with my shawl.

"Yes," Mama acknowledges, "men can be the worst. He's probably just embarrassed—"

"But that doesn't make it okay!" I interject. Why is she taking his side?

"You're right, Sammy, it doesn't make it okay. I grew up with five brothers, I know what they're like at this age, trust me …"

I understand her position here, but brothers are a lot different than boyfriends. If my brother acted this way, I'd just tell him off and walk away. Which, I guess, is a similar description of what just happens not ten minutes ago.

"He should know better, than to project his crappy embarrassed ego on me," I protest. "I don't do that to him, ever."

"But you make mistakes, too," Mama interrupts. "You're no angel, Sammy. Part of loving him is accepting him for his flaws. He's human too, just like you. Isn't that part of your own philosophy? Awareness and acceptance, and all that duality language you subscribe to. Doesn't awareness and acceptance of others, including and *especially* your boyfriend, count, too?"

Damn it, she's right. My mom is so wise.

"I guess you're right," I concede. "But he shouldn't talk to me like that, though. It hurts my feelings."

"You're right, too, honey," she continues. "He shouldn't talk to you that way. There's an opportunity for you to help him be a better boyfriend. Men are like dogs; they need to be trained. You just have to reinforce the behavior with a treat."

I've never heard her say anything like this before, but she's got a point.

I laugh a little, then slowly descend into the abyss of self-deprecating shame. Shame is never productive, yet sometimes we visit it from time to time, on the corner of Self-Doubt and Guilt. What's irritating in this particular scenario is that I have nothing to be ashamed about! I didn't do anything wrong! And yet, here I am, traipsing down the boulevard of broken dreams. I feel shame because I feel responsible for making Ryan upset, which is silly in and of itself, and I feel guilty for speaking up in the first place. The consummate empath's reaction.

Per my personal practice, I allow myself a few minutes to visit Shame on this journey, then turn right onto Forgiveness and on towards Compassion. I have no interest loitering along the crossroads of the punishing pains where Shame lives, inflicted by none other than my own psyche. I'm moving on, to figuring out how to ameliorate this debacle with *mi amor* and make it all better, and of course discuss how we can avoid these types of fights (if you could call it that?) in the future.

But first, it's time for bed. A few minutes after midnight, after a late-night snack of grilled cheese sandwiches and fries with Mama, I head upstairs to get ready for bed. I shower as a means of cleansing, not only my physical body but of the negative ions I feel circling my heart and mind. I put on my favorite Roxy nightshirt, crawl under my down comforter, and slide easily into a coma-like slumber. I'm glad tomorrow (technically today) is Sunday. I can sleep in and worry about nothing. Knowing me, I'll ebb and flow between thoughts of solution to this problem, and watch sports (NBA/NHL play-offs!) on TV with Daddy.

I can still hear Mama watching her favorite John Wayne movie, *True Grit.*

"Young fella, if you're looking for trouble, I'll accommodate you. Otherwise, leave it alone."

CHAPTER TWENTY

I'M JUST... NOT SURE... WHAT IT MEANS?

Ah, the sweet surrender of a Sunday. Daddy picked up donuts for us, a nice surprise. When I asked him the occasion, he said, "I just wanted to do something for my kids."

He surprises me sometimes, how gentle of a soul he is. Maybe it's more so that sometimes I forget. It's nice to have the reminder every so often, if even in the form of sugar-laden, doughy goodness.

Old-fashion donut in hand, I decide to take a walk down along the bayside, since it's such a nice day and all. June can be hit or miss around here. We often endure Mother Nature's June Gloom before summer really gets underway. Typically after the Fourth of July, a staple holiday on the peninsula, the weather noticeably warms and summer graces us with her presence. Most people dub Memorial Day Weekend, or MDW, as the unofficial start of summer. Based on my fourteen years of observations, I disagree.

The Fourth of July historically represents freedom, independence, a separation from hegemonic submission. In Newport, it's that, and a city-wide themed party on steroids. When we were kids, before legislation banned such activities, passersby on bike, rollerblades, and skateboards would carry water guns and spray each other. As fixtures on our patio, we too would sport water guns—in addition to water balloons, and, manned by Daddy, a garden hose. What great fun that was, all but ambushing willing participants in this waterworks of a battlefield that is the public boardwalk. I understand why the city banned such fodder; it can be really unsafe.

I remember this one time two women who were likely in their mid-twenties were riding a tandem bicycle; one was holding what I would learn later to be a beer bong in her right hand. Her friend carried a water gun while steering the bicycle. They happened into the line of fire of Daddy's garden hose, and beer-bong-lady ended up doused from head to toe—her cell phone, which was lodged in the front pocket of her Daisy Dukes, a casualty of the encounter. She had a few choice curse words for my dad (and frankly anyone within earshot).

"If you didn't want to play, why did you show up to the game?" Daddy asked. That shut her up. As a rule, we'd never (intentionally) target someone who didn't have obvious intention to participate in such *water wars*, i.e. held a water gun, water balloons, water jet pack (that was cool). She didn't have a thoughtful retort to respond with. What she did come back with was more of a grunt, infused with some borderline racial slurs.

It didn't faze him.

"I've been in this country a long time," Daddy has said. "Sometimes people don't know what else to do but project their own demons on to others. Sometimes they choose to use race because they don't know what else to do, because their bias gets the better of their brains. That's not a racial thing, that's a human thing."

I'm always surprised when people resort to attacking a

person's ethnic identity as a means of rebuttal. There's something to the science, the science of bias and the deeply rooted wiring of our cognitive capacities, that at least attempt to explain this behavior. When homo sapiens first came into being, evolution nurtured us to perceive those who didn't look like ourselves as an enemy, a foe, a danger. These proclivities still exist in our brains today, hence these unconscious biases we see play out in the form of racial prejudice and other discriminatory behavior. We are capable of adjusting these behaviors, we just need to make the effort to do so, and proactively ask ourselves questions about how we engage with others.

I digress.

As I turn the corner down Buena Vista, my mind oscillates between these July 4th stories and, shockingly, Ryan's own projection of embarrassment and weakness. It's funny, the correlations amongst projection—a distinctly human faculty, unique to those of us who experience consciousness. One might argue, too, that consciousness exists on a spectrum. Someone should perform some studies on that.

Projection is basically the denial of your flaws or hits to your ego, and the consequent attribution of them to others. It's a defense mechanism, to protect our egos and keep them intact. Like most biological instincts, it's a survival tactic. Our environments, our landscapes (both physical and digital) have evolved so much and so quickly that our brains haven't been able to keep up. So we must adjust.

I don't think sharing these anatomical underpinnings on the human psyche will solve the problem Ryan and I are currently managing. Maybe sharing these layers of legacy brain function might help? He's a history buff, like my mom. It might work.

I still haven't heard from him. I realize it's barely been twelve hours, but this shouldn't be a surprise, given my impatient nature.

The fresh air feels nice.

I see some toddlers splashing around in the little inlet under the bridge next to Bay Island. They're shamelessly digging for sandcrabs and feeding the cormorants. (I had no idea what these birds were until I read *Island of the Blue Dolphins* in fourth grade. Cormorants, for reference, are diving birds related to pelicans known for their fishing abilities. They are identifiable by their hooked beaks and fairly dark plumage.) Ah, the blissful ignorance of a child. I don't think I've ever known such felicity; my mind has been as active as an eruptive volcano since the formation of thoughts in my brain have flourished.

At this point I turn around and make my way home. I think Mama is making chicken curry before Game 4 of the NBA Finals. That'll give me some time to read a bit before spending the rest of the day with the family.

Spending time with those you love is important. But one can never underestimate the value of solitude.

I don't hear from Ryan all day. I think about reaching out myself, to test the waters and take a pulse on the degree of brokenness and thus relative reparations that need to be made. Now I'm starting to get worried. I have enough sunken friendships to deal with. My hormones are about ready to throw me into a tailspin of heart palpitations.

But then I remember to breathe. And focus on what I can control.

You can't plan everything, Samantha. Focus on what you can control. And … don't forget to breathe.

I wake up before my alarm Monday morning, which is not unusual, especially when anticipation—wanted or not—cues me.

There's only two weeks of classes left, followed by the last week of the semester, which includes finals, Senior Week, and graduation. Seniors take their finals during the last week of instruction, presumably so they can enjoy the festivities commemorating their high school finale.

Where has this year gone? I'm at a loss. It seems like just the other day Ryan approached me in drama class with the modern-day equivalent of *Do you come here often?"* Yet here we are, ten months, five poems, one prom, and one defining disagreement later: walking a tightrope of tension. At least, that's how it exists in my mind.

Mama drops us off at the pool parking lot just before the first bell. As we pull up to the curb, I see Ryan, almost instantly, standing by his truck, like he's waiting for someone—for me.

He starts making his way towards me, accelerating his gait when he realizes I'm not rerouting my course towards him, even after I notice him. I do this because, honestly, I'm not ready for a conversation and prefer not to be late to class.

At least he's not avoiding me.

"Sam," Ryan calls, as he catches up to me from behind. "How are you?"

How *am* I? Flooded with feelings of sunshine and roses, and you?

I think it but don't say it.

Instead, I go with "Fine, how are you?"

"Good," he answers. "Did you watch the game?" referring to Game 4 of the NBA Finals.

"I did," I reply. "And you?"

"Me too," he says, "gnarly fourth quarter. My team lost but glad it was entertaining."

Insert awkward silence here.

After a few empty beats of muteness, Ryan leads, "Listen, Sam—"

"Ryan," I interrupt, somewhat firmly. "Can we find a different time to talk? I need to take care of a few things before class and the first bell already rang. Can we meet at break?"

He actually looks kind of sad. Now I feel bad.

"Sure," he says. "This is for you, too."

He hands me a folded piece of paper. "I'll meet you at your locker after second period."

"Okay," I manage, feeling like a jerk yet happy with myself for standing my ground. Ever the empath, I shed a few emotion-processing tears before pulling myself together and refocusing my energy on getting to class.

I make my stops and take my seat just before the second bell. I feel justified in enforcing my boundaries with Ryan.

During our warm-up exercise, again something to do with triangles, I pull out the paper Ryan gave me.

Shocker: it's a poem.

Not to belittle the gesture itself; sometimes sarcasm is a coping mechanism. (Like projection, but arguably not as intentionally hurtful.)

It reads:

The love in my heart rages
Like fire.
But at the same time,
It cries tears of pain.
Why is that?
A question in itself that baffles me.
Perhaps,
It comes from fear—
Fear that one day,
I will awake without you in my life.
Or—
That someday you will find someone
Better than I.
But in time,
My trust will be regained
And my forever faithful love for you
Will grow stronger ...
For I will love you always.

I'm conflicted. Is this a peace offering? An apology? Some context would be helpful here. I guess, to be fair, he may have given me more context should I not have dismissed him so readily before school this morning. For now, he can benefit from the doubt. We'll find out in a few hours.

After second period, I make my way towards my locker on the other side of campus. I simultaneously take my time while hastening my pace, eager for this pending exchange with Ryan. I'm curious about what he has to say; my optimism is tempered with some hesitation.

"If you expect nothing from somebody you are never disappointed."

Wise words, Sylvia.

As I turn the corner, Ryan paces to and fro in front of the planter next to the row of lockers where mine is. He looks flustered, in a charming sort of way. He's wearing a plain white hoodie with board shorts and flip-flops, a slight departure from his uniform that usually includes a tee and his turtle backpack. When he sees me, he smiles softly, flickering his eyes to the floor in front of me as though deciding if my gaze will bore holes in his eye sockets upon contact.

"Hey Sam," he greets, raising his right hand almost like a salute.

Wow, he looks nervous.

"Hey, Ry," I return, hoping the use of his nickname signals friendly terms.

"Did you read it?" he asks.

"I did," I reply. "It's beautiful, like all your work," I compliment. "I'm just … not sure … what it means?"

Ryan blinks a few times, then tilts his head as if he didn't understand the question.

"Let me rephrase," I continue. "The poem is well-written and illustrates your feelings very well. But it doesn't give me a clear picture of where we stand following Saturday night's … um … I don't know if disagreement is even the right word …"

"Oh, okay," he concedes. "I can see that."

He pauses, then follows up with, "Where do you think we stand?"

The perfect segue to my soliloquy.

"For starters, Ry, I'd like to hear you say you're sorry for speaking to me the way you did. It really hurt my feelings and made me feel belittled."

He walks over to me and takes my hands into his, and whispers, "I'm sorry for making you feel bad. That was never my intention."

"Thanks honey, I appreciate that. Do you understand why it hurt my feelings? I feel like you projected your insecurities onto me, which is not only unfair but just not … nice …" I let my voice trail off a bit for effect, and also to give him some time to formulate a response.

Time, which he either didn't need or care to use.

"I know, I'm sorry," he offers. "It won't happen again."

He kisses me gently on the lips, sweet and soft as ever, yet this time with an ever so slight hint of guilt and a dash of uncertainty. It's in his kiss, that's where it is.

In the moments following our make-up (?), I'm unsure, still, of whether A) he's truly apologetic and B) if he's aware of his projective behavior. But, love him that I do, I'm willing to give him the benefit of the doubt, at least this time.

Because, fool me once … shame on you, fool me twice … shame on me.

(I hate the use of the word *shame* in this saying, but it best conveys the sentiment in play.)

And so we pick up where we left off, sharing lunch off-campus that day and meeting up later in the evening for a walk down the beach near the jetty by the pier, where we spend so much time—him surfing, and me spectating. There's a comfort in our routine, a peace, a bliss. For now, I enjoy it for what it is: pleasant company.

CHAPTER TWENTY-ONE
FORWARD

Later that week, I run into Alex—literally tripping over her pointy-toe flats outside the ASB office while I'm buying tickets for graduation. (Mama is coming with me to support Ryan during the ceremony.

At first, she's caught off guard. We both are. We haven't had any meaningful dialogue in months. The brief *I'm so sorry, my bad* doesn't count as meaningful either.

"I hope your shoes are okay," I meekly muster the confidence to say. "They seem to have avoided any damage."

Now I'm just being nice, maybe trying a little too hard. There's the empath in me again.

Alex just looks at me, like she has something to say but can't find the words to formulate an intelligible sentence.

"They'll be all right," she submits. Her look is neutral, stoic. She looks like she has perma-resting-bitch-face. She makes eye contact with me, for the first time in I don't know how long.

Progress, I guess.

Or not.

Because with that, Alex continues on her way.

I want to cry, as I so often do. But I don't. For some reason, I am at peace. I don't know if we'll ever be friends again, the kind of friends we once were, the kind of friends that acted as keepers of each others' souls.

The three of us—Alex, Charlie, and I—shared a friendship necklace split into three parts, three words: Best Friends Forever. I won't retire it just yet, if nothing than out of sheer hope, one day, the bonds will be unbroken.

And yet, maybe it's time, time to accept the end of their roles in my story. Maybe it's not. Only time will tell. She can be a beguiling devil, Time. She is my biggest asset as well as my biggest liability. Best to let her be and focus on what I can control.

I share this happening with Ryan, who, true to form, offers his sage wisdom.

"If it's meant to be, it'll be, it'll be, baby, just let it be."

Before we know it, graduation day arrives, with plenty of the pomp and circumstance that the term implies. Seniors are treated like royalty this entire week, with each day dedicated to a senior trip, a senior lunch, and a senior day of hookie—which apparently is school-sanctioned from what I understand? The senior trip is basically a day trip to Catalina Island, a resort-type place less than thirty miles off the California coast. The port, Avalon, is your typical harbor city home to water activities, restaurants, and the like. The senior lunch is an opportunity for seniors to invite their favorite teacher to a hosted meal offsite. It's usually at a golf course country club like Big Canyon. I think this year it's at Strawberry Farms. The day of hookie is self-explanatory; it exists because the administration ran out of activities to sponsor. That's my story and I'm sticking to it.

I, on the other hand, have finals to get through. Aside from Monday, we have what's mysteriously entitled Finals Schedule. Tuesday through Thursday, respectively in this order, where each day, we end at 12:30 p.m.: periods 1-4, 2-5, 6-3. (Administration recently changed flipped the last day so those in sports wouldn't be out of school prior to anyone else. At least they get to sleep in on this day. Interesting timing for parents who drop their kids off at school and work. We never had to consider that, luck us.) One of the perks of finals week, in addition to early-out, is lunch off-site. I don't know what it is about lunch off-site that feels like such a treat. Perhaps it's the choices, the options available, the element of unpredictability. I'll miss getting lunch with Ryan next year. Who knows, maybe he'll come visit me between classes so we can relive the memories and indulge our bellies.

I study pretty thoroughly for each of my finals. I really only have four big written exams: Geometry, French, Biology, and English/Lit. I apply my tried-and-true method in preparation for such tests: study, study, and study some more. It never fails. I have yet to get anything below an A- on any test; so far, this strategy is working for me. It doesn't work for everyone; I recommend A/B testing for good measure.

For dance class we had to choreograph a two-minute routine to our song of choice, which we performed for our class the week prior. We chose a T Swift original, "Shake It Off"—solid eight-counts made piecing the movements together fairly organic. For Dramam we were tasked with lip-syncing a musical number to our movie of choice. We chose "Summer Nights" from *Grease.* I'm shocked to say most kids had never seen it, a classic if there ever was one. Ryan and I played Danny and Sandy, respectively. A couple other kids from our class played members of the T-Birds and Pink Ladies—not including Alex or Charlie, but that goes without saying. I've never heard an applause so loud erupt from The Little Theatre. It's nice to know I have a future as a professional lip-syncer; maybe I should make an appearance on *Lip Sync Battle*. That will go over well with Papa Selim.

Graduation by definition represents birth, dawning, initiation—an ironic departure from the common experiences of its participants, both direct and indirect, which tend to be connotated by termination, a finale, the end. Emotions accompanying these times, from what I've witnessed, tend to be those of closure— sometimes relief, other times, fear. Sometimes excitement, other times, sadness. There's an element of unknown, even for those who have plans, like college, jobs, military service, etc. There's a shift in structure, in frames of reference, that are no longer relevant to daily life. That can be scary, especially for those who like to plan. (I preach to the consummate choir.) This can also be a time, though, when serendipity pays a visit, if you're aware enough to pay attention.

On the grass, under the billowing, white tent on the track and field grounds, march the graduates to their places in the rows of folding chairs designated for their ceremony. I'm sure they've practiced this march at least twice. The almost-navy blue caps and gowns, some accented by floral leis, others by sashes, makes the class look like a choreographed wave of fabric idling in the summer breeze. I see Ryan, focused on his path and smiling, living in the moment, as he should.

> *Be present,*

I texted him earlier.

> *You'll never see this moment again,*
> *so enjoy it*

He takes direction well when he wants to.

Mama and I find seats at the back edge of the grass. I don't have any desire to sit with his parents or his brother, who is a year older than me and thinks I'm too nice. People don't forget.

The ceremony lasts about two hours—including the announcement of each of the 330 kids' names. Honestly, I'm scrolling through Instagram most of the time and zoned out of the presentation after Ryan's name was announced. We clapped and cheered. And then we wait for the caps to be tossed and the pictures to be taken. We agreed we would meet at the fence by the tennis courts after Ryan makes his rounds with his family and friends. Mama graciously waits with me.

Before we meet Ryan, I meet up with Kay. I basically shanghai her as she's walking towards the parking lot with her parents. Don't worry about me, I'm just the overly emotional little sis your daughter pseudo-adopted, unbeknownst to you. I'm devastated she's moving on, too, but in a different way. She's like a mentor to me, the older sister I never had. She brings a light to my darkness, which is more like a shadow than dungyness and dreary. She's going to school at Northwestern, outside Chicago, to pursue her education in film. I will miss her dearly. I consider her to be one of my first true role models. I wish her the best.

I write her a letter (not a poem) expressing these sentiments in some many words.

She tears up a bit, and all she says is, "You are a rock star. I'll miss you too."

Mama and I wait about twenty minutes before Ryan appears, carrying his cap in one hand and a bouquet of lilies in the other.

"We have something to add to your stash," I tease.

I gift him a box of Godiva chocolates topped off with a mini stuffed Snoopy. (Not-so-secret secret: he *loves* the Peanuts Gang.)

"Something sweet and something sappy, just like me," I

lyricize as hand him his graduation present.

"And of course, for good measure," I hand him a card, inside of which is a folded piece of paper with the following poem:

A Day's Commencement

By Samantha Selim

As sunlight departs from our dark days of sorrow,

We hope it will bring back improved feelings tomorrow.

For the sun sets on our broken hearts and our
shattered dreams—

This is the end of life, or so it seems.

But yet, the sun rises—and brushes away our tears,

For a new day is beginning without our past fears.

The sun's rays of light mend our soul's defeat and
pain—

This is a new start to life, for our spirits are regained.

I didn't want this one to be mushy or romantic, but rather uplifting and full of promise—an inclusive salute to the opportunity of the future. We've had high times and low times, the stuff life is made of.

He hugs me tightly, signaling a shared sentiment.

"It's perfect," he whispers. "A perfect depiction of where we've been and where we're going. I'm so lucky to have you."

I blush a little, enjoying this affirmation of love, while acknowledging its fleeting nature.

Mama witnesses all of this, taking pictures to document our moments. The best one is where I put on his cap and gown, which hangs on me like an oversized potato sack.

Before we know it, Ry is on his way to the gym, where he checks in for Grad Nite, the overnight party for the seniors, their last hurrah as a collective class.

I hug and kiss him goodbye; I'll see him tomorrow at Blackie's, where we'll meet following a surf session. He'll regale me with the night's events: who hooked up with who, what DJ they picked, how good or bad the food was. And we'll go forward, as assuredly as the waves crash, as the fires burn.

Let It Rise

Waves crash unchaperoned.
Thrashing, savage, grieving, they moan—
I gaze silent, a witness to this dance in ire,
a stormy, black match of pithy, wet fire.

I feel my soul burn, it churns,
rapping in motion that mimics the ocean,
I feel sadness, a suffering, a delicate
    uncertainty,
a light in my soul that yearns to be free.

Let it rise, let it fly,
can't hide in fear anymore.
Let it rise, let it fly,
in chasing my dreams, I soar.
I am free and I'm finding my way,
Let the waves rage on,
the surf screams and shouts in vain anyway.

Don't be afraid, you have what it takes,
to fight, to survive, to shape your own fate.
Over the moon and across the world,
Your courage sparks the spirit in that
    inimitable girl.

Let it rise, let it fly,
I grow as I spread my wings.
Let it rise, let it fly,
My roots ground me as I pursue my dreams.
Here I go, and here I'll stay.
Let the waves rage on.

My words, they compel strong emotion and
    thoughts,
they prompt introspection, deep feelings—
cold and hot.
My words provoke awareness, acceptance,
    and appreciation,
for all that we are as this life's creation.

THANK YOU!

I am so appreciative of you taking the time to read my book. This novel is very personal to me, and I hope that sentiment came through in my words.

If you enjoyed *If Water Were Fire*, and would be willing to spare just two or three minutes … please share your review of the book on my website:

www.bysarasalam.com

Reviews help me get the book into as many hands as possible, and support my work as an author for the long-term (my dream!).

I'm grateful for your support and look forward to sharing more of my work with you!

ACKNOWLEDGEMENTS

This story has lived in me since the experiences described took place. I never thought I could write a book—a body of work consisting of thousands of words. I always loved to write, but was more of a short-form writer—articles, blog posts, features, you get the idea.

But now that I have, I plan to write books again and again, for as long as I am able to do so.

This novel, my first, is a literal labor of love, inspired by my own life growing up in a safe haven. I was raised by two wonderfully different yet symbiotically soulful humans (my parents), and ripe with thoughts and dreams, with notions of what is and could be.

I can't possibly articulate the gratitude I have for my family, for their support of my endeavors. I'm thankful to the community of people who have offered their feedback, their observations, their wisdom, in shaping the product I have put out into the world for my readers to enjoy.

But most importantly, I am thankful to this community for their role in shaping me. I cannot create without inspiration. I cannot tell stories without experiences to call upon. Thank you to the people who willed me to "keep going." Those two words have inspired more creations than I can count.

Truth is personal. I'm so grateful to have the opportunity to share mine.

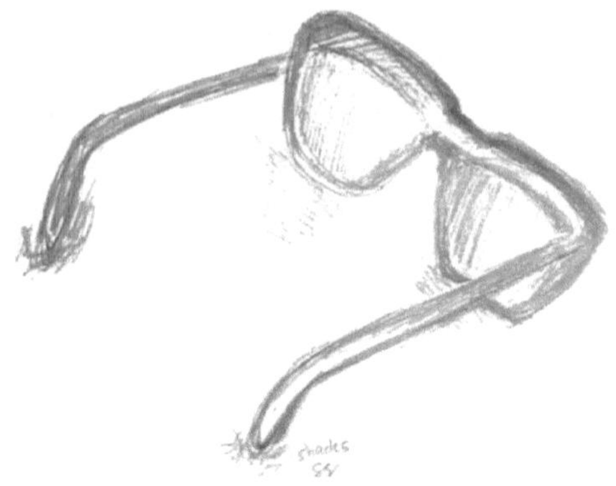

A Note About the Author

Sara Salam is an award-winning author and editor. Published since age 11, Sara writes fiction, nonfiction, and poetry. In addition to her work as an author, Sara spent seven seasons working in professional sports: five with the Boston Red Sox (2013 World Series Champion!) and two with the LA Clippers. During this time, she primarily focused on human resources strategy, including diversity and inclusion, talent acquisition, and professional development. Sara is a proud UCLA Bruin and active in her community of Newport Beach. She enjoys writing, yoga and the beach.

© 2020 Sara Salam

🌐 www.bysarasalam.com

📷 @bysarasalam

▶ Sara Salam

www.ingramcontent.com/pod-product-compliance
Lightning Source LLC
Chambersburg PA
CBHW061617100726
47898CB00002B/695